Hello,
Gorgeous!

Foiled

Withdrawn
Print

Hello, Gorgeous!

Foiled

BY TAYLOR MORRIS

GROSSET & DUNLAP
An Imprint of Penguin Group (USA) Inc.

GROSSET & DUNLAP
Published by the Penguin Group
Penguin Group (USA) Inc., 375 Hudson Street,
New York, New York 10014, USA
Penguin Group (Canada), 90 Eglinton Avenue East, Suite 700,
Toronto, Ontario M4P 2Y3, Canada
(a division of Pearson Penguin Canada Inc.)
Penguin Books Ltd., 80 Strand, London WC2R 0RL, England
Penguin Group Ireland, 25 St. Stephen's Green, Dublin 2, Ireland
(a division of Penguin Books Ltd.)
Penguin Group (Australia), 250 Camberwell Road, Camberwell, Victoria
3124, Australia (a division of Pearson Australia Group Pty. Ltd.)
Penguin Books India Pvt. Ltd., 11 Community Centre,
Panchsheel Park, New Delhi—110 017, India
Penguin Group (NZ), 67 Apollo Drive, Rosedale, North Shore 0632, New
Zealand (a division of Pearson New Zealand Ltd.)
Penguin Books (South Africa) (Pty.) Ltd., 24 Sturdee Avenue,
Rosebank, Johannesburg 2196, South Africa

Penguin Books Ltd., Registered Offices:
80 Strand, London WC2R 0RL, England

Cover art by Anne Keenan Higgins

Library of Congress Cataloging-in-Publication Data is available.

ISBN 978-0-448-45527-3   10 9 8 7 6 5 4 3 2 1

To my niece Catherine,
whose smile alone is more gorgeous than all
the styling tricks in the books—TM

CHAPTER 1

"Mickey, please help!" Lizbeth said, staring at herself in my three-way mirror.

I looked carefully at Lizbeth's long honey-blond hair, which Kristen had attempted to funkify in a cool way. The key word here was *attempted*.

"My hair looks like it's been attacked by the wrong end of a hair dryer," she said.

Kristen had braided Lizbeth's hair into several messy sections, making her normally sleek hair look like it'd been sent through a meat grinder.

Kristen had also twisted another section right above Lizbeth's forehead into a curly lump, like a cat curled up for a long nap.

"It's supposed to be weird," Kristen said, planting her fists on her hips. "Hello, don't you ever read *Vogue*? It's the new look: 'Pretty Ugly.' Right, Eve?"

We all turned to look at Eve, who sat in the corner

where she'd been painting her nails a thick, bright white. Eve was fair skinned with white-blond hair. Playing up that paleness worked well for her.

"Right," Eve said, checking out Lizbeth's hair, her eyes wide. "Pretty darn ugly."

Lizbeth and I laughed.

"Very funny," Kristen said.

"Kristen, I love you like a sister," Lizbeth said. "But I cannot show my face outside this bedroom with this hair. Especially not to Mickey's mom!"

I totally got where she was coming from. My mom is the owner of Hello, Gorgeous!, the best salon in town. She definitely has high standards when it comes to style, and you always kind of want to look your best around her.

I playfully nudged Kristen aside with a bump of my hip and said, "Don't worry. The pro is here."

"Okay, fine. Hey, Eve," Kristen said. "Lemme do your hair?"

Eve, who was blowing on her nails, looked up at Kristen. "Well . . . ," she said, looking at Lizbeth's terrorized head, which I was trying to brush out to look something more like, well, *hair*. Eve had just moved here a month or so ago, so she really didn't know Kristen and Lizbeth that well. I was still getting to know them myself since we'd only recently started hanging out, but at least I had gone to school with them since we were kids. "Okay," she said, pushing herself off the floor carefully, mindful of her nails.

Lizbeth, Kristen, Eve, and I weren't going anywhere tonight. We were just fixing our hair, doing our nails, and having my *first-ever sleepover*, thanks very much. Camping in the backyard with Jonah in elementary school clearly didn't count as a real sleepover. Even though he's been my best friend forever, he is, after all, a boy. He'd never let me style his hair, and believe me, I'd tried.

I was so excited about all the girls coming over that I even took the next day off work to hang out all afternoon with my friends. That was a huge deal, because Saturdays are the craziest days at the salon.

Working at my mom's salon had helped me overcome my shyness and actually start talking to people. I used to watch Kristen and Lizbeth at the salon and at school, and *they* were never shy about talking to anyone, especially not Kristen. She had no problem talking to adults, other girls, and even boys she thought were cute. (She loved embarrassing Lizbeth by calling out to boys Lizbeth liked—especially ones named Matthew Anderson.) Now they were here, hanging out at my house for a makeover-themed sleepover with Eve. Sometimes I still couldn't believe how much had changed in a little over a month.

"Okay," I said after finally getting all the tangles and braids out of Lizbeth's hair. "Do you want to look like you're about to be photographed for a catalog or like you're about to walk down the runway?"

"Runway," she said. "Definitely."

"New York or Paris?"

She thought for a moment. "Paris."

"What's the difference?" Eve asked as she blew on her nails while Kristen combed her long hair.

"Paris looks are edgier than New York." I took the two-inch-barrel curling iron from the side of my vanity drawer and plugged it in. I'd read enough styling and fashion magazines to know that the runways in Paris took crazier, more outlandish fashion risks than anywhere else, even New York—overconstructed dresses with performance-piece hats, accessories, trains. Every outfit was like an exaggerated dream, pure fantasy and fun.

I took a chunk of hair from the crown of Lizbeth's head and locked it in place with a butterfly clip, then took the rest of her hair and brushed it into a low, side ponytail. Then I started back-combing the top.

"So, you guys," Kristen said. "What do you think of this Career Exploration class thing we have to do?"

"I'm vomiting," Lizbeth said.

"I don't know," Eve said. "I think it could be cool, seeing what it's like to work a real job."

"Hello," Kristen said, "we're thirteen. Are we even legally allowed to work?"

Lizbeth shrugged. "Mickey does."

Got that right, I thought. After years of begging, on my thirteenth birthday Mom finally let me start working at her salon as a sweeper.

Here's the deal with Career Exploration: It's a special class that the seventh-graders have to take in the spring where we meet twice a week to talk about jobs. We're supposed to learn about personal responsibility, working with others, and discipline. To achieve this, we have to pick a job to work for six hours a week for three weeks. Lucky for me, I was one of the few people already working.

"I'm thinking of working at the day care," Eve said.

"You're choosing to work with screaming kids who wet their pants?" Kristen said.

"I like kids," Eve said a bit defensively. "What are *you* doing?"

"Oh, me?" Kristen said, like she'd never expected to be asked but was secretly waiting eagerly for the question. "I'm going to work for my rich great-aunt. She has her own radio station and gets to interview, like, all these famous people for her show."

"She owns an entire radio station?" Lizbeth asked. "That's pretty major."

"Yeah," Kristen said. "I know."

"Your turn, Lizbeth," I said, smoothing out the top of her hair after I'd back-combed it. "Where are you going to work?"

"I'll probably just end up working at my mom's law firm doing filing or something equally horrible," Lizbeth said.

I turned her around in the chair to face me and used the pointed end of a comb to piece out the front of her poufed hair, trying to make a tiny, little part.

"Whatever you decide, it has to be by Monday, and if you don't find one on your own you'll have to pick one from that list they have. Jonah said he heard those jobs were terrible, like working for the sanitation department or in a hospital cleaning out bedpans." I put my hand over Lizbeth's brow. "Close your eyes," I said, and sprayed strong-hold hair spray all over her hair. After a couple of minor adjustments, I turned her around to face the mirrors. "So? What do you think?"

Her face said it all—eyes widened, mouth dropped open slightly as the corners turned up. She loved it.

"I love it!" she squealed.

See?

"Mickey, you're amazing!" Eve said.

"Seriously," Kristen said as she finished up Eve's lumpy, loose french braid. "Nice job."

"How did you think this up?" Lizbeth asked, turning her head this way and that so she could catch the different angles in the three-way mirror.

"Sally Hershberger did it once for some celeb at one of the big awards shows," I said.

"Sally *who*?" Kristen asked.

"Only one of the most famous hair-stylists-to-the-stars around," I said. I loved knowing all this stuff my friends had no idea about. "This doesn't look nearly as amazing as what she did, though. A pretty good interpretation, I guess."

"If only we were going out tonight to show it off," Lizbeth said, still admiring her hair.

"We should at least take some pictures," Kristen said, taking out her cell phone. "We can't let these amazing styles go to waste."

After I took several pictures of the new 'dos, I plopped back down on my bed and picked up a thick copy of *Le Look*, a high-end fashion magazine from Paris. It cost a fortune in shipping and only came out twice a year, but Mom and I both loved it. It had thick pages and incredible styles and fantasy-world layouts. I mean, I didn't know too many people who went hiking in stiletto booties and ball gowns like these models did. But one spread really caught my eye.

"Eve, look," I said, holding out the magazine to her. "This looks like you." She sat on the bed next to me.

In one of the editorials, the pictures looked like they were all shot with a silver lens—like black and white except shinier—making the models look like new robots. The models had long white-blond hair with perfectly straight bangs—probably wigs—and wore metallic miniskirts and boots.

"With your pale skin and hair, you would totally fit in," I said.

Eve didn't look flattered. "Um, thanks?" she said. "They look like aliens or something."

"But in a really cool way," I said. "These magazines are about taking the crazy fantasy and working it into something you can actually wear. Like, maybe you wouldn't color your hair silver, but if I added some bright highlights it'd shimmer like the sun was always shining on it."

"If *you* added color?" Eve said, smiling slightly. "Or maybe not."

"But it's easy!" I said. "It's like I've been watching the training video my entire life." But Eve was like, *no way,* so I dropped it.

Looking at her crisp white nails gave me an idea. I got the bottle of black polish I'd used around Halloween last year and a superfine makeup brush I'd never used. "Trust me to do something to your nails?" I asked.

"Of course." She extended her hand to me. I

brushed thin black strokes over the white polish. "So cool," she said. "It looks like tree branches in the snow."

I smiled, watching as Eve held out her hand to inspect her nails, Lizbeth posed in the mirror with her new style, and Kristen carefully read over a how-to style article in another magazine.

The truth? I couldn't believe this was all happening. I finally had friends of the girl variety. They were at my house for a sleepover. *And* they thought I was a styling genius.

I couldn't imagine things getting any better.

CHAPTER 2

The next morning, I had pictured us sleeping in late, then getting up to eat fresh croissants that Dad would pick up from CJ's Patisserie, which was right next door to Hello, Gorgeous! Then, I thought, we could all go to the mall and see a movie or just pig out on fresh-baked cookies and free samples in the food court.

Not quite how it went. We didn't even sleep in. Eve was up by nine thirty brushing her teeth. Lizbeth stretched out of bed, then walked over to the vanity. "What do you think?" she asked, smoothing down her jacked-up hair. "Do I look like I'm ready for the tennis courts?"

"Your hair is about as fierce as your backhand," Kristen said.

"But I have a terrible backhand," Lizbeth said. Kristen smiled. "Oh. Very funny. Mickey?" She pointed to her hair and I went to fix it, starting with the ponytail.

"You're playing tennis today?" I asked as I fastened the hair tie, then smoothed out the top.

"Yeah," she said. "Mom and I are doing the mother-daughter thing. Brunch first at eleven."

"Oh," I said. I was bummed she was leaving, but at least Kristen and Eve and I could still have a fun afternoon.

We all headed downstairs. Dad had, in fact, gone to CJ's and gotten us chocolate, almond, and plain croissants, which we all gobbled up.

"Our last Saturday of freedom before Career Ex starts," I said, even though I usually worked Saturdays.

"I still can't believe we're being forced to work," Lizbeth said. "Seems like it should be illegal or something."

"Hurry and finish," Kristen said to Lizbeth, chugging down the fresh-squeezed orange juice. "We gotta jet."

"You're going to play tennis, too?" I asked.

"Her mom is dropping me off at ballet," Kristen said, picking up almond slivers from her plate with her fingers. "Although the last thing I want to do after eating this awesome pastry is put on a leotard."

"What about me?" Lizbeth said. "I'm about to go eat *again*."

"I'm glad you guys came over," I said, trying to hide that I was disappointed they were leaving so soon. "It was fun."

"Definitely," Lizbeth said. "Next time we'll do it at my house. Maybe we can all go to the club first for dinner in the café."

"Totally," I said.

And then they left. Eve and I watched Lizbeth and Kristen walk down the lawn to the sidewalk and head home. At least Eve and I still had the entire day ahead of us.

"So! I was thinking," I began. "Wanna go to the mall and try on makeup and go to a movie or something?"

"Don't you have to work today?" Eve asked.

"I took the day off to hang out with everyone," I said, feeling kind of lame. "I guess I shouldn't have assumed no one had plans for the day."

"Maybe it's loser-ish to admit this," Eve said, "but I hardly ever have plans, especially since moving here. So I'm totally free for the day. We can still have fun."

"Yeah, totally," I said. "Just us. I can show you the best place at the mall to buy accessories." I'd been wanting to hang out more with Eve—today was the perfect chance.

"Perfect," Eve said. "You don't know this, but I am an expert mall shopper. My plan of attack of the stores is as brilliant as—oh no," she said suddenly. She was looking out at the street. "My mom."

A tan four-door had just pulled up to the curb, and the driver—Eve's mom—waved at us. Eve waved back.

"Is everything okay?" I asked.

"I'm sure it's nothing."

We watched her mom walk across the lawn to us. She had short, spiky hair and wore yoga pants and flip-flops.

"Hi, girls!" she said as she approached us. "Hi, Mickey, how are you?"

"Hi, Mrs. Benton," I said. "I'm fine."

"Mom," Eve said. "What are you doing here?"

Mrs. Benton turned back to Eve and said, "I was just running some errands and I ran into Deanna Keller, the woman who runs the day care center you want to work at. She said she'd love it if you came down today and talked to her. I can take you now before we go visit Nana." She looked at me. "You girls have fun last night?"

"Yes, we had a good time."

"Look what Mickey did to my nails," Eve said, holding her hands out for inspection.

Her mom glanced down at them and said, "Cute."

I wanted to tell her that I had a whole day planned, but it seemed like she wasn't asking Eve if she was ready to leave. She was telling.

"Sorry, Mick," Eve said, and she looked sorry, practically pouting her bottom lip. "Maybe we can do the mall thing some other time."

"Yeah, sure," I said. "No big deal." I tried to shrug it off like it was no big deal, but the truth was, I was beyond bummed everyone had left. I tried to tell myself that my sleepover had been a success, even if it had ended a little too soon. But as Eve got in her mom's car, asking questions about the job, I started to feel a little lonely.

CHAPTER 3

After Eve left, I went back inside to the kitchen for another glass of fresh-squeezed orange juice. Mom was there, dressed for work to classic perfection in a black tailored jacket and pants and black patent heels.

"Morning, honey," she said, sipping a cup of tea like she did on most mornings. "Did everyone leave already? I thought they'd stay longer since you took the day off to be with them."

"Kristen and Lizbeth had plans," I said, sitting down next to her. "And Eve's mom just picked her up. Took her to see about a job for this Career Exploration class thing we have coming up." I told her about the class. "You have to sign a form for me, by the way. It's no big deal since I'm already working at my job. Hey," I said, just thinking of something. "Since they're gone, anyway, I might as well come in today after all."

Mom took a last sip of tea, then stood up. "It sounds like this class is about making mature decisions and sticking by them?" I nodded yes. "Then I think you need to stick with your decision to take the day off to be with your friends. Even if they've all made other plans."

That was the thing about Mom. When it came to her business, she did not mess around.

So I was stuck without much to do. Instead of cleaning my room from the mess we'd made, I decided to go see what Jonah was up to. We have a gate connecting our backyard to his—testament to our respective dads' BFF status—and I walked through it to find him throwing a baseball to Kyle, his friend from school.

Kyle saw me just as Jonah tossed him the ball. It almost clocked him in the head.

"Dude, pay attention!" Jonah called as Kyle went to get the baseball. He turned to me. "Did all your friends go home?"

He knew about my sleepover—I'd told him Friday as we walked to school together. Even though I had *several* new girl friends, Jonah was still the friend I told the most to.

"Yeah, they left," I said. Kyle ran back and threw the ball to Jonah. "Hey, Kyle."

"Hey," he said. He had dark, thick curly hair that

always looked like it was on the verge of needing to be cut. Kyle was cute, but he was always so quiet, at least around me.

"Why'd they all leave so soon?" Jonah asked. "You run them off or something?"

Sometimes I took Jonah's bait, and sometimes I ignored it. I wasn't feeling so great about everyone bailing *and* not getting to work, so I chose to ignore it.

"They had stuff to do. Tennis, ballet, brunch. And Eve went to talk to someone about a job for Career Exploration."

"What's she doing?" Jonah threw the ball to Kyle, who caught it easily in his gloved hand.

"Working at some day care."

I expected him to make a joke about that, like it was lame and boring and typically girlish, but he didn't. He just nodded. "Yeah, I gotta go see the dude at the skate shop about my job."

"So you got the job?"

"Yeah," Jonah said. "Practically."

Practically didn't sound so convincing, but I didn't say so.

"Kyle, what are you doing?" I asked.

"Not sure," he said, throwing the ball back to Jonah. "I'll just take whatever they give me."

"Dicey move," I said.

"Yeah," he said. "I like to live dangerously."

I grinned and watched as they threw the ball a couple more times.

"You want to hang out or what?" Jonah said. "We're about to go play Warpath of Alien Doom. You've barely made it to level two. You could use the practice."

I might have been the master of Warpath of Doom, but the alien version was new. I usually loved playing, but I wasn't in the mood to hang out with guys. I'm all for blowing stuff up on a video game, but today I wanted to bury myself in the pages of my glossy, girly magazines. "Nah," I said. "I'll see you guys around."

"Later," Jonah said.

And Kyle? He didn't say anything. But he did look at me, holding the baseball in his glove. A grin spread across his face before he tossed it back to Jonah. I watched, noticing that his smile and even the way he looked at me—briefly—made him kind of cute. But I would die before admitting that out loud.

I walked back through the gate, thinking about the fun day my friends were having while I was stuck at home—alone.

CHAPTER 4

"I'm not talking to you so don't even try."

That's how Giancarlo greeted me Sunday when I got to Hello, Gorgeous! Not to be biased or anything, but I was pretty sure Giancarlo was my favorite stylist. He just had a way about him that always made me smile—even when he was teasing me. I mean, you just had to take one look at the guy—big, bald, and wearing a white Hello Kitty tee stretched tight over his barrel chest—and you couldn't help but feel happy.

"What'd I do?" I asked.

"And here I thought you were serious about this job." He shook his head as he wiped down his station, readying it for his next client.

"I am!"

"Then tell me why skip out on a Saturday? This Be Gorgeous thing is going through the roof, and we really needed your help yesterday."

This, actually, made me feel really good—they *needed* me. And Be Gorgeous was basically my brainchild. Every Saturday one stylist did a demo, with a little insider tip on how to keep your hair looking gorgeous once you left the salon. How to style it for different looks, what the best products were, that kind of thing. So far it'd been monster successful.

"Sorry, GC," I said. "I had a sleepover with my friends yesterday." Just saying it out loud made me feel better about the fact that they had all bailed early. I had the sleepover—with *several* of my friends—and that was still pretty cool.

"Par*don*," Giancarlo said. "Someone is popular."

In the break room I did the one thing I disliked about my job—I put on my plastic smock. As the salon sweeper, it was part of the uniform and something I'd learned to suck up and deal with. The only dress code for the stylists was that they had to wear majority black or white. Megan, as the receptionist and first face of the salon, could wear what she wanted as long as it was stylish. Mom didn't exactly want her wearing overalls—unless, of course, they were made out of satin or silk and designed by Stella McCartney.

But because of the smock, I'd learned to show

off my style where I could, by wearing cute skirts or pants and shoes and hair accessories, since my shirts didn't really show. Today I wore a black ruffled skirt with a fitted white tee and black flats.

Although my main job was sweeper, I quickly learned when I first started working that my job was much more than that, especially on crazy-busy days like this one. I helped Megan at reception, showing clients to the back to get changed into luxurious batiste cotton robes. Then sometimes I'd have to grab something from the back for one of the stylists—supplies for hair dying (foils, gloves, mixing bowls, and brushes), clips, combs, the works. Oh, yeah, and in between all that I was supposed to keep the floors swept to gleaming perfection. There was always plenty to do.

I swept around Giancarlo's station just before his client arrived—I had to be out of there before she sat down—and Megan motioned for me to come up front.

"Cute shoes," she said. Even in the midst of chaos, she could still dole out compliments and greet clients at the same time. "Could you show Ms. Warren where to get changed? Thanks! Anna, you'll look amazing with the new color. You're in good hands with Devon. Oh, hi, Lily! Here for a facial with Rowan?" Megan was a machine.

"Right this way, Ms. Warren," I said to the ginger-haired woman.

One of the big things I'd wanted to gain from working at the salon was the ability to, you know, *talk* to people. And I had done that in a major way. (See: *sleepover*.) But talking to people I didn't know—especially adults—still made me freeze up with nerves. I was trying, though.

As I led the way to the changing rooms, I thought of what Megan had said to Ms. Warren about getting a new hair color and how Ms. Warren still seemed kind of nervous about it.

"Even if Devon does a terrible job," I said to Ms. Warren, "you'll still look better than now."

As soon as I heard myself say the words, I realized what I'd done. I didn't need to hear Ms. Warren's little gasp of breath. I didn't need Violet, the salon manager who had a no-nonsense look—all pixie cut and glittery blond—shooting me evil glances, either. Only she did.

"Ms. Warren, you always look gorgeous! And don't worry, Devon is one of our top stylists. She'll take great care of you," Violet said as she nudged me out of the way, ushering Ms. Warren to change.

"No, that's not what I meant," I said, but Violet led Ms. Warren away from me as if I'd just busted out with a case of Tourette's.

Great. I'd been back at work for about thirty minutes and already I'd messed something up. I refolded the towel Violet had tossed aside and prepared to face her when she came back.

"Mickey, honey." Violet sighed as she came back for the towel.

"I didn't mean it like that," I said. "Honestly."

"I know, but be careful what you say. She's coloring her hair for the first time ever. Don't make her feel bad about herself."

"I didn't mean to. I just meant Devon is so good that even if she were having a bad day Ms. Warren would still come out looking beautiful."

Violet gave me a stern look. "I know. Now back to work. Okay?"

Deflated, I got my broom and looked for spots to sweep.

I tried to sweep away the bad vibes while I dreamed of a day in which I ran my own Hello, Gorgeous! Maybe I'd open a salon in Boston. Or maybe New York City. Or Paris or Milan or London or Singapore. Endless—when my mind ran, the possibilities were totally endless.

"Mickey!" Devon—Goth-chic with jet black hair, blunt bangs, and matte red lips—was deep into Ms. Warren's coloring job. As always, Devon was retro-cool in high-waisted capri pants, a white shirt tied at the waist, and a red bandana headband. "Could you get me some more foils from the back? I'm almost out."

"Sure," I said, watching for just a moment as Devon dipped a dye-soaked brush into the bowl she held containing the new coloring for Ms. Warren's hair. She took a section of her hair and placed a square of foil beneath it, then brushed the color on. Finally she folded up the foil toward her scalp, securing it in place. Devon saw me watching and gave me a little wink. I smiled, then headed back to get the foils. She made it look so easy. Section, brush, fold, done!

Before I could get far, though, I got a happy surprise—Lizbeth came into the salon.

"Hey!" I said. "What are you doing here?"

"Nails," she said. "I'm the only one who didn't do mine at your sleepover."

Lizbeth and Kristen had been coming into the salon as clients since about the fourth grade. Mostly they got manis and pedis, but they also got haircuts. Their hair always looked better than mine, even though I had learned to style from a pro.

"I'll get you a bottle of water, okay?" I told her. Another perk of the salon—free beverages.

"Thanks, Mickey!" Lizbeth said. She settled into the couch while she waited for Karen, the manicurist, to finish up with another client.

I could have gotten a bottle from the side table that

held all the drinks, but I wanted to get my friend a cold one, so I went to the refrigerator. On my way back up, Devon looked at me expectantly. Oops! I was supposed to get her those extra foils.

"Forget something?" she said, holding her hands out to the side, one of which held the small plastic bowl with the hair-dye mix.

"Oh, sorry," I said. "I just have to deliver this and I'll get them."

She dipped her brush into the bowl and, with the bowl still in her left hand, brushed the dye on another section of hair.

Devon's station was right behind Karen's manicure station, where Lizbeth was now seated, so at least I didn't have far to go to deliver the water. "Here you go," I said to Lizbeth.

"Thanks! Have you seen this color before?"

I looked at the bottle she held—a sheer, pale purple. "Sea Glass Haze, yeah," I said. "It's really pretty on. Light and springy." Devon cleared her throat behind me. I made an *uh-oh* face to Lizbeth, then smiled. "Gotta go!"

I quickly turned back toward Devon, but she'd moved closer to the manicure station. I was halfway to facing her when we collided, my body slamming into hers so hard I squeezed my eyes shut.

"Oh my gosh!" someone said.

The wind had been knocked out of me but I was glad I hadn't fallen to the floor. When I got my bearings, I saw that the bowl of dye Devon had been holding had gone flying in our collision. It splashed on the floor, and all I could see was red all over Mom's pristine, cream, and *expensive* marble floors.

"Are you okay?" I said to Devon, who had a stunned look on her face. I kept one eye on the floor.

"I'm okay," she said.

Knowing this, I practically dived to the floor with the rag I had in my smock pocket, desperate to clean it up before Mom saw it and freaked. As I wiped up the dye, heels clicked past me—Mom's spiky heels. I realized no one had stopped to help me. That's when I heard the commotion behind me at the manicure station. I turned to see what was happening. It wasn't pretty.

The woman sitting next to Lizbeth had her hand over one eye as Lizbeth stood next to her, pouring water from the bottle I'd brought her onto a napkin. Mom was there, trying to see what was wrong, but it was Lizbeth who put water on the woman's eye and patted her shoulder.

Still on my knees, I realized the dye had splattered to the mani station and into the woman's eye. A freak accident. As Lizbeth and Mom ushered the woman—who was probably going blind at that very moment—past me, Mom looked down at me and said, "What are you doing down there?" She looked at the rag in my hand, and I got what she meant— how could I worry about the floor when a woman's eye was burning into her skull?

Lizbeth, Mom, Karen, and Devon all rallied around the poor woman as they leaned her back into one of the sinks to flush her eye out. Tears welled in my own. What had I done this time? Had I really hurt that woman? A slow, familiar panic seeped through me. It wasn't so long ago I accidentally started a rumor about Devon making some poor woman go bald. When she found out what I'd done, I'd had this same feeling. I watched, paralyzed, as Lizbeth said something that made the woman laugh while Mom ran water gently over her eye.

"You okay down there?"

Giancarlo knelt beside me with a spray bottle of floor cleaner, spritzed the area where some splatters had landed, and helped me wipe it up.

"Giancarlo," I said, the words barely coming out of my mouth. "That woman—is she . . ." My chin started quivering as if an 8.0 earthquake were in effect right on my face. I'd made mistakes before, but I'd never *physically* hurt anyone.

"Hey, hey," Giancarlo said, looking me in the eye and resting a baseball glove–sized hand on my shoulder. "Look at you. Calm down, girl. It's not that bad." I tried to steady my breathing, but it was impossible. "Mickey, look at me. She'll be fine. Believe me. She's not the first person to get a little hair dye in her eyes."

I sniffed and said, "She's not?"

He nodded. "It happens sometimes. Usually not outside beauty school, but it happens. Come on," he said, heaving himself up. We'd gotten the floor pretty clean—you couldn't see a single smudge. "Let's pick up this other stuff." He picked up the dye bowl and brush from the floor and placed it on Devon's trolley next to her station. I stood up and tried to pull myself together. Giancarlo took me by the shoulders as if trying to steady my shaking. "There's no crying in the salon. We are all beautiful here, all the time. Okay? Take a deep breath and pull yourself together."

The thought of facing the woman who could only see with one eye was frightening, but I knew he was right. I had to be mature and own up to what I'd done.

Mom came back up to attend to her client, who had waited patiently for the drama to end. When she passed by me she leaned in close and said, "We'll talk about this later." My stomach dropped.

"Is she okay?" I asked, my voice quivering again.

She turned back to me. "You should go ask her yourself."

The woman was now sitting up in the chair at the sinks, wiping the water from her face. Violet and Lizbeth stood beside her, and the three of them were talking as if nothing had gone wrong, as if she was just back there to get her hair washed. I walked up to her on shaking legs.

"Um, hi," I said. She looked up at me, one side of her hair wet from the rinse. "Um, your manicure looks really nice. I mean, um, I'm really sorry."

"It's fine," she said, then dabbed her twitching eye. I wanted to cry again, but held back, remembering what Giancarlo said.

"I'm really sorry. Let me know if you need anything. Sorry."

Another smooth performance by Mikaela Wilson! So eloquently spoken! I couldn't believe what I'd done.

Devon was wiping down more spots near her station when I approached her. "Devon? Are you sure you're okay?"

She looked at me, her blunt bangs still hanging perfectly below her red kerchief. "I'm okay. A little rattled, though. Are *you* okay?"

I felt relief knowing she wasn't mad and that she was even a little concerned. We'd come a long way from rumors about making clients go bald. Devon was cool, but I'd learned the hard way that you didn't want to cross her. "I'm okay. I just feel stupid."

"Everyone messes up sometimes. Jill—that's the woman's name—is fine, and I'm sure she'll come back again. So don't sweat it, okay?"

That made me feel better—still guilty, but better. "Thanks, Devon."

Things finally settled down. Jill left, twitching her eye at me and loaded down with on-the-house shampoo and conditioner as well as gift cards for a new manicure and style on the house.

"Hey, Mickey?" Megan called from the front. She set a box on the accessories counter, took out a pair of scissors, and cut open the top. "Want to put these out for me?"

"Sure," I said. I barely noticed the accessories as I took them out of the box. (Okay, that's a lie. Even in my shame from physically harming a client I noticed how cute the military-inspired striped barrettes were.) As I put them in the case, Lizbeth came up. Karen, who was totally scolding me with her eyes, had finished Lizbeth's manicure—also on the house. Mom had given away a lot of business today, all because of me.

"So," Lizbeth began as she watched me put an old-fashioned tortoiseshell comb in the display case. "That was kind of crazy, huh?"

"I can't believe I did that," I said. "Don't get me

38

wrong, I'm very good at messing things up, but that was a whole new level for me. I feel awful."

She smiled a pity smile at me. "She's fine," Lizbeth said, picking up a black crystal barrette and inspecting it before I put it in the case. "Seriously. I think she was kind of overreacting."

I sniffed. "Lizbeth, you're too nice. I'm sure it was pretty uncomfortable and borderline scary. I was practically bawling. You, though—you were so good with her. You were the calmest one here. Calmer even than my mom. She was ready to rip my head off."

"It's funny. She mentioned that, too—how calm I was, I mean. Not about the head-ripping," Lizbeth said. "She said that any employer I get for Career Ex would be lucky to have me because I'm quick on my feet. Or something like that," she added as if the exact words didn't matter. Judging by her flushed cheeks, though, I was pretty sure that she was flattered.

"Did you tell her how utterly excited you are about working at your mom's firm?" I smiled.

"Yeah, like, so excited," she said. "Well, I guess I better get going."

"Okay," I said. "Hey, your nails look really good." The sheer purple was subtle and looked great against her skin.

"Thanks," she said, looking down at them. "See you tomorrow at school."

As I watched Lizbeth leave, I had a funny feeling in the pit of my stomach—it probably had something to do with what I'd done to Jill. Or maybe it had something to do with the fact that I was still messing up at work, and I felt Mom's eyes on me more than ever. Mom didn't let screwups work in her salon, and I hoped she didn't decide I was one of them.

CHAPTER 5

That evening, Mom stood before me in the kitchen in classic angry-mom stance: feet set wide apart, hands on hips, scowl on face.

"Mikaela."

Oh, if I had a fiver for every time she called me by my full name.

"I thought you were done with these sorts of mistakes," she said.

The kitchen table was set for a lasagna dinner. On a normal day, I'd be ready to devour half the casserole dish. Today . . . not so much.

"Mom, it was an accident. I'm sorry."

"I understand that, Mickey, but I don't want word getting around that this kind of thing happens in my salon. Do you understand that?"

It was like someone hit the replay button: Mom was disappointed in me—again. She was angry with me—again.

"I know," I began. "I'll be more careful and not ever mess up one more time." I thought of Jill's twitching eye and oh, brother, the tears started welling up in my eyes. "She's okay, though, right? The woman—Jill?"

Mom sighed, shaking her head. "She's fine, honey. Thank goodness Lizbeth reacted so quickly, though. She was great."

Mom sat down at the table as Dad brought over the just-mixed garlic butter.

"You girls hungry?" Dad asked.

"It looks amazing," Mom said, and it did. It's just that my stomach was in knots from all that had happened. "I was thinking," she began. I stood, waiting for her to finish with *of sending you to boarding school in Switzerland to make sure you don't ruin my business.* Instead she used the toe of her shoe to push out my chair. "Relax, honey," she interjected. She could obviously tell how stressed I was. "Have a seat. Look at this great dinner Dad made us."

I sat down. Maybe she wasn't going to fire me. Of all the things I thought she'd say next, though, I never thought she'd say this.

"I was thinking," Mom said again, "of Lizbeth and your Career Exploration class. I'm happy to see you making so many new friends."

"Yeah. I'm glad I'm making new girl friends, too.

It's like Jonah's cool," I said, "but he never lets me do his nails."

She smiled. "I asked Lizbeth what she was doing for the class, and she said she was working at her mom's law office, but honestly, she didn't seem very excited about it."

I took a slice of bread and smeared the garlic butter on it. Taking a big bite, I said, "She's not, but she doesn't know what else to do. If she doesn't have something by tomorrow they'll make her choose from this horrible list of jobs, and she could end up doing something worse than filing papers in some office."

"Well, I was thinking," Mom said, "what if she worked at the salon? You'd have to stay focused on your work there, but wouldn't that be fun for the two of you?" When I looked at her I saw a little glint in her eyes.

"Really?" I asked. Not only was I relieved that I wasn't being shipped off to Europe, but I was incredibly excited about what she was saying. Me and Lizbeth, working together? My mind raced with all the fun we'd have. I loved my job already, but if one of my friends was there, too, it'd be even better! We could walk to work together from school, go to CJ's on our breaks to get hot chocolate and iced cookies, and be the first to test the new nail polish colors—legally this time, of course. Not long ago I had "borrowed" some new samples and given them to Kristen and Lizbeth. When they went missing, everyone freaked, Mom found out, and I got in huge trouble. But I was past all that now and totally responsible.

"Be Gorgeous has really taken off," Mom continued. "We're busier than ever, and Saturdays are almost more than we can handle. I could use the extra help. What do you think of having Lizbeth do her assignment with us at the salon?"

A grin spread across Mom's face. And then, I couldn't help myself—I sprang from my chair and threw my arms around her neck.

"I'll take that as a yes," she laughed.

"Mom, thank you!" I said.

"Just remember," she began, "this isn't an invitation for you to slack off. If there's any indication that the two of you are goofing around—"

"I promise, I swear, I *assure* you there won't be!" I said. "Can I please be excused to go call Lizbeth and tell her?"

Mom said okay, and I took off running for the stairs to my room. As soon as Lizbeth answered I said, "Oh my gosh, guess what?"

She laughed. "You've just been nominated to host your own styling show?"

"I wish," I said. "No, listen. It's about Career Ex." Lizbeth groaned. "What do you think," I said, then paused for dramatic effect. "Of doing your assignment . . . at Hello, Gorgeous!?"

"Wait," Lizbeth said. "Are you serious?"

"Totally," I said. "My mom just told me. So what do you think? You want to? You do want to, don't you?" In my mind I couldn't imagine any sane person not wanting to work at Hello, Gorgeous!, but maybe Lizbeth was secretly excited about doing legal stuff with her mom.

"I don't know," Lizbeth said. "I was really looking forward to making photocopies for hours on end."

I laughed, relieved. "So you're in?"

"Most definitely," she said.

"Awesome," I said. "We're going to have so much fun!"

I told her my mom would call her mom later to work out the details, and when we got off the phone I felt the disaster of the afternoon slip completely away.

※※※

The next morning, after Jonah crashed breakfast like he normally does, we started our walk to school.

"So," I said as we walked down the tree-lined street. "How'd Saturday go at the skate shop? They going to let you work there?"

45

"Well, it's, you know . . . ," he stammered. "It's a little complicated and, um . . ."

I had a feeling things at the skate shop weren't as solid as Jonah had thought. "I thought you had the whole thing locked in?"

Jonah groaned, shoulders slumping. "I went there and the owner told me that about ten guys had already stopped by looking for a job that was already taken."

"I thought it was *you* who'd taken the job? You said it was all set."

"Can we please not talk about it?" he said, tugging on his backpack.

"Now you're going to get stuck with whatever's on that list," I said. "You might end up working for, like, the funeral home, putting makeup on dead bodies." I shivered. I loved playing with makeup, but that was a bit much—even for me.

"Actually, that'd be kind of cool. Is that one of the choices?" Which is just what you'd expect Jonah—or any guy, I suppose—to say.

❋❋❋

Later that morning, three homeroom classes gathered in the Little Theater—a small assembly hall at our school—to officially kick-start Career Exploration. When I got there, I spotted Jonah sitting with Kyle—they had the same homeroom so they probably came in together. There weren't any seats next to them, but the row behind them was practically empty. I sat down and thumped Jonah on the back of the head.

"Hey," he said, turning to face me. Kyle did, too.

"What's up, Mickey?" Kyle asked.

For some reason I became tongue-tied. Probably because of that crazy thought I had—you know, the one where I thought Kyle was cute? It made me want to say something clever back to him, but all I could get out was, "Nothing."

"There's your friend," Jonah said, nodding behind me. I was grateful for the distraction from those five seconds of total awkwardness of Kyle looking at me *and* talking to me—whatever that was about.

I turned to see Eve walking down the aisle, her white-blond hair pulled back in a slick ponytail.

"Hi!" She sat on the end seat beside me. "Are you guys excited? Is it nerdy that I am?"

"Yeah," Jonah said, but he was smiling. Those two had a weird something between them. It was clear that they liked each other—as in *liked* liked—but so far they hadn't admitted they liked each other. Then again, I didn't exactly know the rules of how these things worked.

"Your nails still look amazing," I told Eve, inspecting them. "Not a single chip."

"I've been really careful with them. I actually told my mom I couldn't rinse off the dishes because it might interfere with my manicure."

I laughed. "Did she go for it?"

"No, but she gave me a pair of these hideous yellow gloves to wear, like I was about to handle nuclear waste."

Soon, Lizbeth and Kristen came down the aisle. I motioned for them to sit with us.

"Hey, co-worker!" I said to Lizbeth as she and Kristen squeezed past me in the row. I know it was a dork moment, but I was really excited about her working at the salon. We'd work, but it was still going to be fun.

"Hello, gorgeous!" she said back as she sat down.

Ms. Carter, my homeroom teacher, stepped up to the mic. Kristen crossed her arms tightly over her long-sleeved Madras top and slumped in her seat on the other side of Lizbeth. "Good morning, students," Ms. Carter began.

"Is she okay?" I whispered to Lizbeth, because I couldn't help but notice that Kristen didn't look as excited as the rest of us.

"Job," she said back.

"We're very excited to start our Career Exploration program and are sure you'll find many benefits to learning about the real world." Ms. Carter used air quotes for *real world*, as if it might not truly exist.

"Are you so excited about working at the salon?" I asked Lizbeth, keeping my eyes on the stage. Teachers roamed the aisles, looking to fulfill their life's goal of sending a kid to detention.

"So excited," she said.

This was going to be the best—and easiest—class assignment *of all time*.

"Now, we don't expect you to come up with a career path in the next three weeks." Ms. Carter chuckled. "But we hope this program will give you a feel for what it's like to be out in the work force. Remember, you're just *shadowing* someone at the job to get a feel for what goes into a work day. Could I get a show of hands for those who have not yet secured a position?"

I didn't have to look too far to see some hands go up—Jonah's and Kyle's. I could see Jonah's disappointment in not getting that job at the skate shop just by looking at the back of his head. He loved skating as much as, if not more than, his video games.

"Great!" Ms. Carter clapped as if this were a wonderful turn of events. "Come up after the assembly and we'll hand out assignments. And for those of you who have jobs, make sure you get the permission forms signed by your parent or guardian and your new employer no later than Friday.

"You will give two reports on your work experience," Ms. Carter continued. "The first report will be a five-page written report you'll submit about halfway through to show your progress, what exactly you're doing at your job, and what you hope to achieve. The final report will be oral and will summarize your work experience. These reports together will be the bulk summary of your grade. Now, for those of you who need to choose a job from our list, come on up."

Jonah sighed. "Save us a seat in the caf. And maybe an extra plate of fries."

As we moved into the aisle to shuffle out with everyone else, we ended up right behind Matthew Anderson and Tobias Woods—Lizbeth's and Kristen's crushes, respectively. Last week they were all supposed to be at the same table at a fund-raiser at the country club. Lizbeth's parents had invited the boys' families to join them, and she and Kristen (after a small tiff) had been beyond excited about spending a fancy, dressed-up evening with the guys. But it was all for nothing. Although the guys' parents showed up, the guys didn't. Now Lizbeth and Kristen were making an extra, pointed effort to totally and completely ignore them. I don't think Matthew or Tobias noticed, unfortunately.

I could see the way Kristen's and Lizbeth's bodies

went rigid when we got behind the guys. Because there were so many of us, it was a slow shuffle out of the Little Theater. I nudged Kristen, knowing she was never afraid to speak up.

"If you're still upset about them not coming to that fund-raiser, then just say something," I said to her. "Just ask what happened."

I wasn't surprised when Kristen, who was always more outspoken than Lizbeth, took my advice. Or maybe she was just tired of wondering why they didn't show.

"Hey, Woods," she said to Tobias, giving him a little shove in the shoulder. He turned to look at her. "I hope you feel good about the choice you made."

"What choice, Campbell?" Tobias said.

She rolled her eyes as if her cryptic talk were oh-so-clear. "The fund-raiser last weekend at the country club? You two numbskulls left me and Lizbeth to fend for ourselves while all our parents argued over the best brand of lawn mower, and the band played Michael Bublé. It was the worst night of my life."

"Oh, that," Tobias said. "We were totally broken up about missing Michael Bublé. His fault." He pointed to Matthew, who was the preppiest guy known to the Berkshires. He wore jeans without a single rip, tear, or bleach mark; leather shoes like my dad wore; matching belt; and a polo shirt. If you liked that type—which Lizbeth did—then he was pretty cute.

"You guys were there?" Matthew asked, looking at Lizbeth.

She looked down at her feet but managed to say, "Yeah."

"Too bad," Matthew said. "If I'd known you were going to be there . . ." He stopped himself, then said, "A guy my dad golfs with gave me tickets to the ball game that afternoon. We couldn't say no."

"Sorry, ladies," Tobias said, "but when the Red Sox call, you gotta go."

We all filed through the door and into the hall, making our way toward the cafeteria. I walked beside Eve, who gave me a secret smile at the way Lizbeth accidentally-on-purpose ended up walking beside Matthew, her arm inches from brushing his. We followed behind them.

"Did you get a good job?" Matthew asked Lizbeth.

"Yeah, an amazing job," she said. "I'm working at that salon on Camden Way called Hello, Gorgeous! What about you?"

"Working at the country club pro shop. I might get to do some stuff on the golf course, too. Tobias scored the best job, though," Matthew said. Tobias, who walked ahead of them with Kristen, raised his fist in the air. "He gets to be a bat boy for the Sox for their next three home games. Scored it last weekend at the game."

"It's called planning ahead, children," Tobias said. "Learn it."

"And knowing the right people," Matthew said. "Admit it."

"Plus, I'm doubly awesome because of my age," Tobias said, ignoring Matthew's last comment. "The MLB says you can't be a bat boy until you're 14, but I'm getting an exception because of my awesomeness."

"What's MLB?" Kristen asked.

"Major League Baseball," Tobias said as if that were the dumbest question in the world.

"He has to stay in the dugout," Matthew told Lizbeth. "But it's still really cool."

When we all got to the cafeteria the guys started off toward their own table, a few over from where I'd been sitting with the girls. "I'll see you around," Matthew said.

Once the four of us were settled at our table with our lunches, Kristen leaned her head in toward us and said, as if she were letting out a long breath, "Oh my gosh, they are so cute!" We all started laughing. "I mean, okay, I'm still bummed they weren't there for the fund-raiser. I keep thinking about how amazingly the night could have gone if they had been. But it seems like they had no idea whatsoever that we'd be there, so there's no way we can take it personally," Kristen said. "Right, Mickey?"

The girls thought that because I'm best friends with a guy, I'm somewhat of an expert on them. Which was hardly the case. But I did like being asked.

"Yeah, totally. No guy would rather go to some dress-up dinner than a baseball game. Like, ever, in the history of boys."

Lizbeth and Kristen nodded, satisfied.

"You're looking better after seeing Tobias," I said to Kristen. "You looked pretty upset this morning."

"Ugh, that," she said. "My aunt's radio station is not exactly the kind of radio station I thought it was."

"Then what kind is it?" I asked. I looked at Lizbeth, who had her head down, stifling a giggle—unsuccessfully. She practically snorted. "Come on. What kind is it?"

Lizbeth grinned. "All talk, all the time. *All boring.*"

Kristen sighed. "This great-aunt of mine has this radio station in a dingy, little office that is practically an outhouse, and all these old guys sit around all day talking into an old mic about old people stuff."

"She's your aunt and you didn't know this was what she did?" I asked.

"Great-aunt, and obviously no, Mickey, I didn't know."

"So-orry," I muttered.

"I just thought it would be something cooler, like a fancy satellite station where I could have, like, just an hour a day to play whatever music I wanted or interview cool people—like maybe Rihanna or Katy Perry—and basically get some decent but fun experience. But no. I'll be getting coffee and Metamucil for a bunch of oldies while they talk about their jacked-up digestive systems," Kristen said.

Jonah and Kyle came and sat down at our table. Last week I'd sat with the girls a couple of times and with Jonah and Kyle a couple of times, but on the days when we had assembly together right before lunch, we kind of just stuck together for lunch, too.

Jonah slumped against the table, burying his face in his hands. Kyle tried to suppress a smile as he dug into his sack lunch.

"What are you so happy about?" I asked. Kyle shrugged and basically looked more animated than I'd ever seen him, his face flushed and sort of lit up. "Tell us!"

"I'm working at the firehouse, that's all." His cheeks stretched into the kind of smile that, if his face had allowed it, would have gone all the way to the industrial microwaves in the back of the caf. For the first time I noticed he had a crooked tooth, one that leaned slightly over the tooth next to it like the two were fighting to be in front. Kind of cute.

"Okay, *that* is cool," I said of his firehouse gig.

He nodded, taking a bite of his sandwich. Through a mouthful he said, "I know. I just hope there's a fire when I'm there."

"Kyle!" Eve said. "Don't say that."

"Oh, sorry," he said. "You know what I mean."

"Your turn, Goldman," I said to Jonah. "Tell us what you got."

"Yeah, Goldman." Kyle grinned at me, then looked back to Jonah. A tiny *zip* went through my stomach. "Tell them."

We waited for Jonah to remove his face from his hands. He took a deep breath and said, "I have to work at the antique store on Camden Way—Loretta's Treasures. It's bad enough my mom drags me in there sometimes. Like I want to *work* there?"

We started laughing and Kristen said, "Maybe talk radio isn't so bad after all."

"The worst part," Jonah said, "is that I have to work in the toy department. This Loretta chick must think we're all seven years old or something."

"It could have been worse," Kyle said. "You could have gotten that job at the baby clothing store."

I laughed, picturing Jonah selling bibs and onesies. Kyle smiled back at me. I liked that he was getting in on the convo. He usually didn't, at least not while I was around.

As Jonah and Kristen moaned about their jobs, I asked Lizbeth, "Did Mom say what you're doing at the salon?"

"I'm only working on Saturdays. She said something about helping out in the front with Megan."

"Really?" Working the front of the salon was a big deal. It means you're the face of Hello, Gorgeous!, giving clients their first impression of the salon when they walk in. Mom had taken her time finding just the right person in Megan because the job is so important to her.

When I realized I hadn't said anything, I said, "It's just that that's a huge deal, working the front."

"It is?" Lizbeth asked, looking slightly panicked.

"Yeah, but it just means that my mom has a lot of faith in you. That's a good thing," I added. Even though she'd be working with Megan, I could still show her the ropes, and we could definitely still have fun on the job.

"Okay," Lizbeth said, and her face seemed to relax a bit. "I just hope I don't mess up. Mostly I'm excited because I think it's going to be so fun."

"No fair," said Kristen, who'd been listening in. "You guys are so lucky. I'm going to be stuck in some tiny office with the elderly while you guys are glammin' it up."

"That just means you'll have to schedule a treatment or something so you can come see us," I said.

"Maybe," Kristen said.

I pictured myself and Lizbeth ruling the salon while our friends visited. In my head, it looked like the best job in the world. Which, of course, it was. And it was about to get better.

CHAPTER 6

"So you're pretty excited about Lizbeth working at the salon, huh?" Jonah said as we walked home.

I smiled. "How'd you guess?"

"Because you had that same stupid grin on your face through most of lunch that you have on now," he said, but not in a mean way. Jonah just knew me very well. Better than anyone.

"It's going to be fun," I said. "Even though Mom is already telling me to make sure we work and don't goof off. Besides, it's not like we'll be glued to each other—I'm all over the place doing my job, and Lizbeth will be up at reception." I pictured Lizbeth and Megan up front, working together and greeting clients. "It's a little weird . . ."

"What is?" Jonah asked.

"Not weird, I guess," I said, thinking. "I know it doesn't seem like a big deal but . . . I don't know." I guess I didn't know what I was feeling.

"You feel like she's on your turf or something?"

"It's not that. I was just surprised to hear that Mom put her at the front of the house. It's an important job," I said. It wasn't even the job I wanted; it was just that Mom had put her faith in Lizbeth so quickly. "But I am excited about her being there. I really think we're going to have fun."

"Then don't make a big deal about it. I mean, it's not like she's going to be so much better than you that your mom fires you and keeps her," Jonah said.

❋ ❋ ❋

"Hey, Mickey," Devon said on Wednesday. She had just walked a client out, her halter sundress making her seem sunny despite her tough-girl attitude. She'd had tons of new business since Be Gorgeous began. People loved her funky style and the way she was incapable of giving a simple cut. Every style had to have that something extra to make it special and unique. "I hear we're getting some fresh meat here on Saturday."

I swept the small pile of hair into my little dustpan. "Yeah. My friend Lizbeth."

"A little friendly competition, huh?"

"Not really," I said. Another thing about Devon? She was a genius at finding anyone's Achilles' heel.

"Isn't she the one who helped out with Jill last weekend?"

"Yeah," I said. "How do you think she got the job?" I knew Devon was trying to tease me, but I wasn't going to let her get to me.

I did a full sweep around the salon, making sure I got every last piece of hair. I had to do an amazing job every day, but especially today, because it was my first day back since the dye incident. I had to make sure Mom knew that it had been a freak accident and it wasn't dangerous or something to have me work at the salon.

"Mickey," Devon called as she seated her next client over at her station. "We need a second opinion." I walked over to her, wondering if this was her way of showing me she wasn't upset about the dye-spewing accident. I'd gladly take it. "What do you think of these colors?"

Devon held two swatches near the woman's eggplant-colored hair. That color was so three years ago, if it was ever at all.

"I want something a little brighter," the woman said. "Not so dark and gloomy."

I thought carefully about the colors before me, considering how they'd look with her skin tone and what I guessed was her natural color showing through her roots.

I pointed out a rich red with something like sun-kissed highlights. "This one," I said. "It'll look good,

I think. Like you've been getting some sun at the lake."

"Um, well, I'm not sure," the woman said.

"Yeah," Devon agreed. "I think it's a little brassy for your skin tone. Too harsh. I think maybe this one would work better. What do you think?" she asked her client.

After the woman agreed to the color Devon had chosen, she told me thanks and sent me on my way. I felt embarrassed for giving bad advice, but I tried not to let it get to me.

Later, Megan asked what I thought of a new barrette they were thinking about ordering—a large clip that kind of looked like a brooch with gold-toned rhinestones.

"I like it," I said. "It's pretty. Retro."

Megan held it in her palm, inspecting it. Then she put it up to my head and looked again. "I don't know," she said. "Kind of grandma-ish."

I was embarrassed by Megan's comment, like I had suggested the ultimate in bad taste.

For the rest of the night I stuck to the one thing I had actually become good at—keeping the floors clean. At least that was something that was pretty hard to mess up, even for me.

That is, until Lizbeth started working.

CHAPTER 7

Saturday I went with Mom to the salon early to help open up. She said Lizbeth was supposed to be there half an hour before opening, and I wanted to be there to make her feel welcome. I even asked Mom if we could pop into CJ's for some welcome-to-work muffins and donuts.

"Thanks for coming in early, sweetie," Mom said as she flipped on the lights and booted up the front computer.

"I want to be here when Lizbeth gets here," I said, setting down the bag from CJ's. "Show her around and stuff."

"I'm sure Lizbeth will appreciate that. Just make sure you remember your job," Mom said.

Why did she always have to squash the enthusiasm? Mom didn't get that I was there early to go above and beyond and all that rah-rah employee stuff. I should have been getting extra credit, not a warning.

The stylists began arriving to set up or just drink coffee and gossip, each looking more fabulous than the last. Giancarlo, whose goal in life was to never be outdone, wore a pink paisley blazer with a tight white shirt and black jeans. When Violet arrived, she looked even more polished and pressed than usual in a form-fitting black dress with a soft gray cardigan cinched with a black belt. Even though she was the salon manager and a top stylist, today was her first Be Gorgeous demo, and the girl looked ready to blow them all away.

I'd worked at Hello, Gorgeous! long enough to know that it wasn't just about hairstyle, but about style in general. Some stylists didn't even like doing their own hair, but they always managed to look superglam with tousled hair and killer clothes. After all, they were selling beauty.

I arranged the pastries in the back break room just so, wishing I had thought to pick up a welcome sign like the staff had done when I first started. Giancarlo put his bag in one of the cubbies, and when he reached for the lemon poppy-seed muffin, I slapped his hand away.

"Hey!" he said, holding his hand as if I were a dog who'd just bitten him.

"Sorry, GC. It's just that they're for Lizbeth on her first day. I wanted her to have the first pick of the batch."

"Fine," he said, trying to act injured. He couldn't keep it up, though, because he added, "What a good friend you are."

The front door chimed, and I knew it had to be her.

"She's here!" I said, nudging Giancarlo aside to make my way to the front.

As Lizbeth walked into the salon I noticed two things immediately—she looked adorable and terrified. She had curled her hair in big, chunky curls that looked like they'd been styled by Violet herself. Too bad about the outfit, though, at least the top—black, off-the-shoulder, and shredded down the center with a white tank underneath. It was cute, but it wouldn't show once she put on the smock.

"Hi!" I said, making big strides across the floor to greet her. "Welcome to the team!"

"Hi, Mickey," Lizbeth said, clutching her hands at her waist.

"Are you excited?" She looked petrified.

"Yeah, I mean, I'm really excited."

I took her clammy hand and said, "I'll show you to the back so you can put your stuff away."

As we walked to the back, I pointed to the stations of each stylist and our facial expert, Rowan, who all greeted her with a friendly hello. I gave a special introduction to Devon, though, because of the recent flying-dye incident.

"She's working here now," I told Devon, even though she already knew.

Devon turned her green eyes to Lizbeth and said, "Make sure Mick here shows you where Chloe stores the sample products for staff to test."

Lizbeth, who suddenly seemed nervous to be talking to an adult, said, "Sure! I mean, I love swag!" I led her away before she could babble something truly dorky.

"This is where we keep our stuff," I said as we entered the break room. "And—surprise! I got you some essential breakfast goodies to help get your day started." I stood next to the plate of pastries and pushed them toward her. "You get the first pick."

Lizbeth looked warily at the plate. "Maybe in a bit? My stomach is a little upset."

"Nervous?" I said, and she nodded.

"It's my first job and all."

"Don't be nervous—it's going to be fine! You'll see. And just so you know, when there's free food around, you gotta be quick. It goes fast." She took another look at the box and shook her head.

"If you're sure," I said, a little bummed my welcome pastries were a bust. "Let me give you the tour. This is where we take breaks, store extra towels and products, eat lunch, hide out when things get crazy, all that stuff. It's our all-purpose room."

"Your mom said Saturdays are pretty busy," Lizbeth said.

"Insane," I clarified. "But I'm sure you'll do fine. I'll be here the whole time. Now, last but not least." I reached into the top cubby. "The one bad thing about the job. I know, it's awful, but it's a must." I handed the black smock over to Lizbeth.

"Ugh," Lizbeth said. She took it from my hands as if I were giving her a pile of used hair extensions.

"I know. Mom almost had a meltdown when she saw I wasn't wearing mine on my first day."

"It's like"—she rubbed the plastic between her fingers—"a shower curtain."

We both laughed. "Now you know not to wear such a cute shirt to work since it's a tragedy no one will ever see it."

"Well, if this is the worst part of the job, then I think I'll be okay."

"You *will* be," I said. "I'm here to help, and of course Megan is, too. We should probably go up front and get you ready."

She slipped on the smock with the appropriate sneer on her face as I laughed, and then we headed out to reception where Megan was going through the schedule.

"Welcome, welcome, welcome!" Megan cheered when she saw Lizbeth. Megan looked pretty as usual in a shimmery purple tank and skinny white jeans. "We're so happy you're here. It's going to be fun. You'll see!"

Lizbeth blushed and said, "Thanks. I'm really excited, too."

"Lizbeth, you're here!" We all turned to see Mom walking up to reception, her zipper-front heels click-clacking as she came. "Welcome, sweetie, to Hello—oh no. No, no, no, no, *no*. What in the world are you wearing?"

We all froze, watching as Mom looked Lizbeth over. Poor Lizbeth looked like I felt—panicked and vomitous. How could we have messed up already?

"No smock for you," Mom told her.

Lizbeth looked to me and I said, "But I thought . . ."

"Lizbeth, you're working the front of the salon. Our greeter and receptionist need to convey the feel of the salon while being professional. Wear something fun and cute and you'll be perfect."

Lizbeth unsnapped the smock and handed it to Mom.

"Ah, much better!" she said, inspecting Lizbeth's outfit. "Perfect for the front of the house! Now, Megan, you've showed her how the phones work and where we keep the drinks and the robes?"

"Just getting to it," Megan said.

"Great! Well, welcome, Lizbeth. Let me know if you have any questions."

"Thanks, Mrs. Wilson," Lizbeth said.

"Feel free to call me Chloe. Here, Mickey." Mom handed me the smock to take away. She turned her eyes back to me and said, "Did you get those towels from the dryer folded? We're opening in ten."

"Just getting to it," I said. I don't know what I'd been thinking. I really thought the smock was something Mom made me wear because I wasn't a real, full-time employee. I took it to the back, crushed it into a ball, and shoved it into the cubby.

It was fine, really. So Lizbeth didn't have to wear the dreaded smock, so what? I was here to prove myself as a stylist, no matter what I wore—even if I had to wear plastic.

CHAPTER 8

Ah, yes. First day on the job—I remembered it well. The panicked feeling that I was doing everything wrong, the silly mistakes I made, the embarrassment of messing up in front of so many people.

I had to admit, Saturdays were tough days to start at the salon, what with Be Gorgeous and all. The demo didn't start until a little later in the afternoon, so Lizbeth had some time to either get into a groove or flip out and go home. I kept an eye on her as I swept the stations, once or twice getting called upon (read: snapped at) to pay better attention.

Later in the morning, I stole a moment to go to the front to see how she was doing. We hadn't gotten to hang around each other like I'd imagined, and I hoped she wasn't miserable and bored—or overwhelmed.

The lounge was full of women waiting patiently,

reading magazines and chatting with one another. I did a little sweeping near the manicure station right behind reception so I could say hi to Lizbeth and make sure she wasn't freaking out or messing up too badly. But what I saw wasn't a panicked first-day-er, but someone who looked like she was totally in her element.

"Hi, Ms. Adams!" Lizbeth greeted a woman who had just come in, her hair wrapped in a green and white silk scarf. "How are you?"

"Lizbeth, darling, hello! I didn't know you worked here," Ms. Adams said as she untied her scarf, revealing gorgeous salt-and-pepper hair in a tidy chin-length bob.

"It's for a school project. You're here to see . . ." She looked at the monitor. "Piper! She's just finishing up. Can I get you something to drink?" The phone rang just as Megan walked a lady to the back to get changed.

"Yes, thank you. Sparkling water, dear. I haven't seen you playing tennis at the club lately."

"I'm starting up again after this school project. Hello, Gorgeous!" Lizbeth said, without even taking a breath as she picked up the phone. While she chatted with the person on the call about which day she wanted to come in, she reached back to grab a bottle of sparkling water off the side table, twisted off the top, and handed it to Ms. Adams—all with a smile on her face.

I couldn't believe it. It was like she'd been working here for five hundred years.

Where were the first-day-on-the-job blunders like I'd had? Where was her—what did Mom once call it? Her *learning curve*? Unlike me, it seemed that Lizbeth was a natural.

"Step on it, kid," Piper said to me as she came up front to see off one client and greet Ms. Adams. She grinned to show she was joking, but I also think she sort of meant it because, truthfully, I'd just been kind of standing there, watching the wonder that was Lizbeth.

As I swept across the salon, I overhead Violet say to Giancarlo, "What about the new girl? She's amazing."

"I know," Giancarlo said. "A natural. Kid's got a future."

Traitors! I thought. *What about* this *natural's future?*

The fawning over Lizbeth died down a bit as people crowded into the salon for Violet's styling session. Back when I sat for Devon for the first-ever Be Gorgeous, she'd showed me—and the crowd, which included a local newspaper photographer—how to gently style my otherwise unruly hair. The tips she'd given me—how to hold the blow-dryer as if it were an iron and always use products sparingly—had totally turned my once *don't* into a total *do*. A do 'do!

Chairs were set up in the center of the salon, and Lizbeth helped pass out postcards with a coupon on the back for ten percent off a cut while I swept the other stylists' stations. They had clients during the demo but kept the noise down—even Giancarlo managed to avoid breaking into spontaneous song.

Violet's model was Cheryl, a regular who had tight curls in her long hair. After Lizbeth had passed out postcards to everyone, Megan allowed her to sit and watch the demo. I watched from the side while waiting for Giancarlo or Piper to finish so I could swoop in and sweep their stations.

"Some people's tendency is to put a lot of product on tight curls like this to keep them from frizzing," Violet said. "But you don't want to end up with crunchy curls, so go easy."

Like Devon had done with me, Violet showed how to style Cheryl's hair for a simple daytime look and how to keep it healthy and tamed. Then she finished it off by doing an upsweep for nighttime.

It already felt like a long day. My feet were starting to hurt and just standing around was killing me.

"Since she's the salon owner's daughter, I know she has great taste. What do you think, Mickey?"

74

"Huh . . . ?"

Violet looked at me, and the rest of the crowd turned in their seats to stare. At me.

"Do you think her hair type would benefit from an olive oil treatment?"

Violet waited. The guests stared at me, waiting. Suddenly, replaying in my mind on a loop was Wednesday, when I was asked my opinion on a hair color and an accessory. I'd botched both, which had sucked the confidence right out of me. And now, all these people were watching and waiting for my genius response.

"I'm not sure, but I think it might help."

Don't breathe a sigh of relief just yet. It wasn't me who spoke up, but Lizbeth.

"But I'm sure Mickey knows better than I do," Lizbeth said, looking my way with wide, uncertain eyes. My entire face was paralyzed, and I just stared back at her.

"Yes," Violet said, turning to look at Lizbeth. "Everyone, this is Lizbeth Ballinger, a new team member who is doing her Career Exploration project with us. And how lucky are we?" Everyone smiled and some clapped with approval while Lizbeth blushed.

After the demo was over and everyone cleared out, Lizbeth came over and said, "Are you okay? I didn't mean to get all in your business, but you looked a little stuck."

"Yeah, no," I said. "It's fine. I totally spaced."

Mom came up to us and said, "Great job today, Lizbeth, really. You should be very proud—you survived your first day, and it was an especially busy Be Gorgeous day at that!"

"Thanks," Lizbeth said.

"Well, you've both had a long day," Mom said, looking at me as well. "You can head on home if you're ready. Lizbeth said you girls have to write a report about the first part of your work experience?"

Lizbeth nodded. "I've already started making notes."

"Wow, very proactive," Mom said. "How about you, Mick?"

I had to stop myself from rolling my eyes. "Mom. I grew up here. I've already been working here for over a month. How hard can it be?"

Mom gave a look that said she wasn't so sure it'd be that easy, but I chose to ignore her.

"Well, thanks, Chloe," Lizbeth said. "I guess I'll go see if my mom's here yet to pick me up. Thanks again for letting me work here. I can't wait for next Saturday!"

"Well, we can't wait to have you back next week, either, Lizbeth," Mom said.

We got our stuff, and I walked outside with Lizbeth to wait with her for her mom to come. I felt embarrassed about a first-timer having to bail me out during the demo, but I couldn't let it get to me. It'd been a fluke, anyway.

"Okay, tell me honestly," I said. "What'd you think of the job?"

"I like it," she said. "Once it got busy and I didn't have time to be nervous, it was fun. I'm really glad I'm getting to work here."

"Me too," I said.

Her mom pulled up, and Lizbeth picked up her bag to leave. First she turned to me and said, "You're not mad at me for talking during Violet's demo, are you? I didn't mean to be a kno—"

"No," I said, hoping I sounded genuine. I mean, because I *was* being genuine. "It was fine. I don't know what happened. Just sort of froze up. I needed someone to reboot me."

She smiled. "Okay. I felt bad but if you're sure—"

"I'm positive," I said. "Thanks for helping me out."

"Thanks for helping *me* out," she said. "I'd never have survived without you."

I knew she was just being nice, especially on that last part, but I appreciated it, anyway. I was still sure we'd have fun at the salon, just maybe on a less busy Saturday.

When I got home that night I tried organizing my vanity. I couldn't shake the icky, pathetic feeling I had in the pit of my stomach. The clean-up wasn't helping, though. Another fail. I was racking them up left and right.

I walked across the backyard to Jonah's to see if he was around. Demolishing him in Warpath of Doom always made me feel better, but his mom said he wasn't home.

"He's at his new job," she said. "And you might want to steer clear when he gets home. He was not happy about going."

I went back upstairs to my room to call Eve and see how her job was going—and maybe vent a bit about mine as well. She said it went well and that she walked out of the day care without a single booger smeared on her jeans by a kid. Then she asked me what working with Lizbeth was like.

"I don't know," I answered, sinking into my bed. "I mean, good. It was good."

"You don't know or it was good?"

"It's just weird working with a friend, I guess. Lizbeth is great. And everybody is, like, *so* in love with her. It makes me feel like I'm the worst employee Mom ever hired since I make a million mistakes a day," I said.

"Okay, hold it right there," Eve said. "Because now you're talking crazy. You are not a bad employee—you were born to work at a salon. And not just because you practically have pomade running through your veins."

"Um, ew," I said, and Eve laughed.

"I'm just saying," she said. "You were probably just having an off day or something."

"Try an off week."

"Fine," she said. "But get over it quick. You're great at styling and we all know it. Okay?"

Maybe Eve was right—I was overreacting and maybe even feeling sorry for myself. So I had stumbled and a couple of my suggestions had fallen flat. It happens, no big deal.

I still had to get up the next day and style again.

CHAPTER 9

Things were back to normal on Sunday—I was the only teenager working at the salon. Within minutes of putting on my smock and picking up my broom, I felt like my old self again. No weird vibes, no feeling anxious, just happy and relaxed to be in my second home.

Mom was at her station in the very front—it was the closest station to the waiting lounge, reception, and the door. Being the owner and all, she liked to keep a close eye on things, especially at the front of the salon. She was working on a woman who was getting her blond hair highlighted so it was a bit brighter than normal. Her name was Renee and she'd been coming to Hello, Gorgeous! for years. Mom mixed the color in the plastic container, which was a weird milky-honey color. I knew that when it was applied to her hair it would be a sunshiny gold or something.

"Not much is going on, Mickey," Mom said. "Want to take a break?"

"Okay," I said. "Can I watch?"

When I was a kid hanging out at the salon, I used to love watching Mom style. Now that I was an employee I had less time since I was, you know, doing my job. But I loved the easy way Mom worked a head of hair. She made it seem so effortless.

"Sure, sweetie," Mom said, and then surprised me by saying, "Pull up a chair." I gladly pulled an extra chair from the lounge and watched as Mom carefully but easily put a panel of foil under a small, fine section of hair to protect the scalp. Then she brushed the color on the section of hair on top of the foil. Finally, she folded the foil up into a tight little rectangle.

"So, Mickey, are you going to be a stylist someday?" Renee asked as Mom sectioned off another area and brushed on the color.

I nodded. "Definitely."

"She's on her way," Mom said, and I grinned from ear to ear.

Just as Mom was finishing up, the door chimed and there was Eve. I wondered what she was doing here.

"Hi," I said, getting up from my chair. "Do you have an appointment?"

"No, I was just in the neighborhood. I hope it's

okay—I won't stay long."

"It's fine," I said. "I haven't officially taken my break yet, so I can hang out. What are you up to?"

"I'm on my way to meet my mom at the diner."

"Let me see if Mom will let me walk down with you," I said.

Mom was definitely in a good mood, so I gave it a shot. "I expect you back in ten minutes," she said.

Out on the sidewalk, we started down Camden Way.

"So how was work yesterday?" I asked, feeling very mature and like an adult.

"It was fun," Eve said. "The kids are *so* cute. This class assignment is going so fast. I've worked two days and it's already time to start writing the report. Have you started?"

"Not yet," I said. "But it's not due until Friday."

"It's *five pages*," Eve said. "That's a lot, especially since most of us have only worked a day or two. Have you ever written a report that long?"

"No, but come on. Me, writing a report about Hello, Gorgeous!? It'll be like writing in my diary. Cake."

"If you say so," she said. "Oh, I have an idea! Since they're due on Friday, do you want to celebrate by going to the mall Friday night? Especially since I had to bail on you last weekend."

Up ahead, I could see the firehouse on the left and Loretta's Treasures on the right. I wondered if Kyle and Jonah were at their jobs today.

"Yeah, that sounds great," I said. "Should we invite Lizbeth and Kristen?"

Truthfully, I still didn't know all the rules of girl friends. Would it be rude not to invite the other girls to come with us? It didn't make sense that we'd have to do *everything* together, *all* the time, but I also didn't want to hurt anyone's feelings.

"Let's just have it be the two of us, if that's okay. Maybe afterward you can sleep over and then my mom can drop you off at work."

"Sure," I said as if I'd been thinking this all along.

Just then we came up on the firehouse. "Should we see if Kyle's working?" I figured if Eve could drop in on me then we could drop in on him, right? I mean, we did all sit together at lunch.

But Eve looked across the street and said, "Or we could go see Jonah. I think he's working."

"Is he?" I asked.

"Well," she said, "he texted me earlier saying he had to work."

"Eve!" I said, giving her shoulder a little shove. "You guys have moved to texting? When did that happen?"

"I don't know," she said, but judging by her grin

she knew exactly when. "Sometime this week, I guess. But it was just something about Warpath of Doom originally."

"You *so* want to go see him, don't you?" I asked.

"You *so* want to go see Kyle, don't you?"

"No," I said, but I couldn't hide the blush from flooding my face. I immediately started smiling.

"Mickey!" Eve said. "Do you like Kyle?"

Full on, third-degree blush on my cheeks. They were on fire. "*No.* I mean, I don't know," I said. I *had* been noticing new things about him—like his smile and his crooked front teeth. "He's kind of cute. Don't you think?"

"In that adorable kind of way," she said. "So—do you want to stop in and see him?"

"No way!" I said. "I just might think he's cute, that's all. Why—do you want to stop in and see Jonah?"

She shook her head no. "Let's forget about seeing the guys. I think we're both too chicken," she said, and I agreed. "I should go meet my mom and you should get back before you get in trouble."

"Fine," I said. I stopped and she kept on toward the diner, where I could see her mom waiting out front. "See you tomorrow!"

I started back toward the salon. I couldn't help but peek into the firehouse as I walked past, just to see if I could spot Kyle. A mustached firefighter caught me looking and I took off running. But I smiled the whole way back to the salon.

CHAPTER 10

"How's that report coming along?" Mom asked a couple of nights later at dinner. "Lizbeth said she's got half of hers done."

"She talked to you about her report?" Just how chatty had those two become?

"She stopped by the salon after school today to ask me a few questions about running the salon and the general operation of it."

"Well my report is going to be just fine," I said, which was pretty much true. I know everything there is to know about the salon. Practically.

"Just remember," Mom said, spearing an asparagus, "you have to keep your grades up if you want to stay at the salon. I expect you to get a top grade on this, Mickey," she said, looking at me closely. "So don't take this report lightly."

"Mom, I'm *not*," I said. Maybe I hadn't started it

yet, but that didn't mean it wouldn't be great. So great, in fact, that it would be better than Lizbeth's. Not that I was competing or anything.

That night, I thought about my report. I sat in front of the computer in Mom's home office and tried to think of how it should begin. With the first time I was carried into Hello, Gorgeous! in my mom's arms as a baby? Or on my thirteenth birthday when I started working? I also wasn't sure if it was fair to talk about all the work I'd done before Career Ex started. But maybe that's what would make my paper better?

I turned off the computer and decided to think it over.

In between dinner, homework, cleaning my room, and working very hard to create the perfect wild-but-styled look on my own hair, I wondered what Lizbeth's paper would be like. What exactly had she and Mom talked about, and for how long? I got this image of them sipping tea together at CJ's while Mom advised Lizbeth on how to be the best business owner in New England.

And then suddenly, it was Thursday. The night before the report was due. I'd done exactly zero work on it—I hadn't even decided how it would begin. I needed to focus, and I needed to make sure my report was better than Lizbeth's. I'm not competitive or anything, but the salon's, like, in my blood, so mine *should* be better. Plus, I grew up there, whereas Lizbeth had been there for maybe two days. No way could she get a better grade than me.

I sat in Mom's home office that night and pounded it out as best I could. We had to write about what we were doing and what we had learned so far. All I could come up with was stuff like don't blind the customer and don't give lame advice on color. But I was pretty sure Ms. Carter wouldn't accept that as an insightful answer.

As much as I loved the salon and my job, I found it hard to get five whole pages out of it, so I bumped the font up one point and pinched the margins in slightly. The change was so subtle Ms. Carter would never notice.

The next day's boring assembly featured an edge-of-your-seat speech by some guy who worked in . . . *finance*!

When we woke up at the end of assembly we all filed out and headed into the cafeteria for lunch. Eve and I walked together, with Lizbeth and Kristen slightly ahead of us.

"My mom said she'd drive us to the mall tonight," Eve said. "Pick you up at six?"

I looked nervously to Kristen and Lizbeth, hoping they didn't hear. I was pretty sure they hadn't. "Yeah, sounds good."

"Save me a seat in the caf," she said. "I left my lunch in my locker."

In the cafeteria I dropped my bag on the seat next to me for Eve. I tried not to look at Kyle, who I just happened to notice looked kind of cute in a gray T-shirt. I don't know what it was about that shirt that looked so good on him, but it totally did. When he caught me looking, my eyes automatically darted down to my PB&J. Instant mortification set in. He probably thought I was zombied out, sitting there staring at him like some mental patient. What next? Drooling? Real classy.

"That assembly was almost as brutal as my job," Kristen said. "This week I had to go with my aunt to interview a guy about soil. A live radio interview about *soil*, people. *So* glad it's Friday. We should all do something this weekend."

"I got plans with my boys," Jonah said, punching Kyle in the shoulder.

"Yes," Kyle said, and they bumped fists. "Total rampage."

"You guys are nice and all," Kristen said, "but I wasn't inviting you. Girls only."

Kyle looked to Jonah and said, "Then maybe we *should* come."

Was it just me or was Kyle less quiet than he used to be? I wondered briefly if he was speaking up more to get my attention, then thought that was kind of egotistical of me. Still, I had to admit that it was cute when he spoke up. He was actually pretty funny.

"We should have a makeover competition," Kristen said, ignoring Kyle's comment. "Everyone can come over to my house tonight and we can see who can style their hair the best—like, the most outrageous—and Mickey can be the judge."

"Oooh, I'm in," Lizbeth said.

"I'm in," Jonah joked. I rolled my eyes at him.

"You in, Mickey?" Kristen asked. "It'll be fun!"

A gentle wave of panic had been rising over me since talk of weekend plans started. Eve had said she wanted our night at the mall to be just us, so I took that to mean I shouldn't tell Lizbeth and Kristen. Otherwise they'd be mad we didn't invite them, and that was the last thing I wanted.

"I, uh," I said, trying to think of some way to respond. "I promised my mom I'd help Violet with product inventory."

"Lame," Kristen said.

"I could come in and help if you want," Lizbeth said. She looked so eager with her wide eyes. "I know it's not my regular day, but it might help my final report if I can see how the other business stuff is done. Do you think your mom would mind?"

"You're seriously asking if you can work on a

Friday night?" Kristen said. "You must be sick in the head. Or really love that job."

Lizbeth smiled. "I do love it."

"Um, that's okay," I said. "Mom is barely letting me do it because it's such an important job." Wow. I sure could make counting bottles of polish sound like counting money from the register.

"Oh," Lizbeth said. I could actually see her shoulders slump she was so bummed.

"Too bad. I guess you'll just have to do that thing you've been doing every weekend since we were six— you know, hang out with your *best friend*?" Kristen teased, tugging on Lizbeth's arm.

Eve sat down then and opened up her sack lunch.

"How about you, Eve?" Kristen said. "You down for hanging out with me and Lizbeth tonight?"

"Can't," she said. "I have plans. But maybe next weekend." No lies, no further explanation. She made it seem so easy. Maybe it was.

Kristen then launched into a story about Harry, one of the radio personalities, and how he keeps calling her "doll face." Jonah and Kyle had shifted away from us and were talking about the Red Sox's upcoming game. I ate my PB&J, feeling the peanut butter stick to the back of my throat.

I just hoped Lizbeth and Kristen didn't find out we went to the mall without them.

CHAPTER 11

When I jumped in Eve's mom's car that evening, I had almost forgotten about not inviting Kristen and Lizbeth to go out with us and how guilty it made me feel. I was mostly excited about going shopping—even if I barely had any money to spend.

"Hi, Mickey," Mrs. Benton said, pulling into the street. "How are you?"

"Good, thanks," I said, buckling myself in in the backseat.

"Cute outfit," Eve said, turning from the front. "You always look good."

"Really?" I said. I did think my outfit was perfect mall attire—a plaid sleeveless shirt over a white tank with a black miniskirt. "Thanks."

"I look blah as always. Especially my hair."

"Please. That necklace is so cute," I said of the long, thin gold chain with a funny, little octopus charm. "I can fix your hair when we get there, if you want."

"I totally want," Eve said.

When we got to the mall, Eve's mom said we should text her when we were about ready for her to come get us. As Eve and I walked through the entrance, I dug my emergency bottle of pomade out of my bag and rubbed some on my fingers. "Here," I said, and she faced me as I used the product to tuck her hair behind her ears with a slick shine. "There," I said, handing her a mirror. "Subtle but simple."

"Genius," she said. "You are totally genius."

I smiled, putting the mirror and pomade away. "So how do you want to do this? Want to just start at one end and go to the other?" Eve looked at me like I'd suggested we check out the latest trends at Baby Gap. "What?" I said. "No good?"

She pulled her white slouchy backpack up higher on her bony shoulders—accentuated by the white spaghetti-strapped tank she wore—and said, "You may be good at styling, but I have a better system when it comes to the mall."

"Okay," I said. "As long as we hit everything."

"Including the food court, at least once."

I liked her thinking.

"The most important part of this," she said, as serious as if we were about to set out on an uncharted exploration, "is where we start."

"Well, I know one thing for sure," I said, pointing to Vitamin World across the way. "I'm in desperate need of some fish oil."

Eve looked at the store and said with equal seriousness, "For that occasional irregularity, right?"

"Ew!" I said, and we both laughed.

Her cell phone twittered, and she took it out of her purse. As she read the text on the screen, a smile spread across her face.

"Something good?" I asked, curious.

She texted something back and quickly put it away. "It's nothing," she said, but I could tell she was trying to hide a smile.

Inside Vitamin World, we strolled down rows filled with bottles of vitamins with strange names and made jokes about them.

"Let's get some ginkgo biloba," I said, looking at the bottle. "It says it's good for brain power, and we have that English test coming up."

"I'm thinking of buying this glutathione," Eve said. "You know, for my oxidative stress."

We browsed past calcium magnesium zinc tablets and other strange things. "Do you miss your old school?"

She paused before saying, "Yeah. I guess. I still talk to my friend Marla on IM a lot. She's going to visit me this summer. And it's not like Ridgeley is that far away," she said. Ridgeley was where she used to live.

"That's cool," I said of her friend's visit. "It must have been hard moving away, though."

Eve ran her slim hand over plastic bottles that promised stronger health and a longer life. "I was mad at first, but now that we're here I can see how much Nana loves having us around. And I like being around her." She shrugged and said, "Plus, I don't want to be the whiny kid who complains about moving and having to make new friends."

"I would probably be that kid, and I don't even have many friends," I said. "I know you have your friends back home, but if you ever want to talk about stuff . . . I don't think I could offer good advice, but I'm really good at nodding my head and making concerned and understanding faces. See?"

She laughed as I demonstrated. "Thanks, Mickey. I might just take you up on that."

We rounded the end of the final aisle of Vitamin World and made our way back out into the mall.

"Last chance to get some shark cartilage to support your creaky joints," I said. "It's on sale!"

"Shoot, I just stocked up last week."

We left laughing, and I knew that right there in Vitamin World we had become true friends.

Next we went to Monique's Accessories, where we put on sunglasses that were too big for our faces and dug through piles of scarves, wrapping them around our heads and necks like we were cruising around in a convertible in the 1950s. Then we headed to the food court for a non-dinner dinner.

"We eat, but no real dinner foods," I explained. "This is my contribution to our mall experience."

"So I can't order Chinese food?"

"You can. Just so long as you only order egg rolls and fortune cookies."

"I love this kind of dinner," Eve said.

I got garlic knots and Eve got spicy curly fries. We sat at a table in the center, dug into our food, and started talking.

"Oh my god, look at him," Eve said, nodding to a guy about our age sitting with a bunch of boys and scarfing down a chili cheese dog like he was part of the Fourth of July hot dog eating contest. "Cute, right?"

"Mmm, I love a man with chili stains on his chin," I joked. "Yeah, he's okay. He kind of looks like Kyle." I immediately felt mortified—why had I brought up Kyle?

"Yeah, but Kyle's cuter," she said with a huge grin on her face. "I mean, if you like that type. So. Do you like Kyle or something?"

It was embarrassing to talk about, even with Eve. "Maybe. I'm not sure. I've known him ever since he started school with us in fourth grade. He's just always been Jonah's quiet friend. I never really knew what to make of him, but lately he's been a bit more talkative. I like it. But that doesn't mean I want to, like, be his girlfriend or anything." I took a bite of another garlic knot.

"Not yet, anyway," Eve joked. She grew quiet, then said, "Ya know before, when I got that text?" I nodded. "It was Jonah."

"What'd he want?" I asked, then immediately knew the answer. Like, duh.

"Nothing," she said. "We've texted a few times and messaged online. Nothing big."

I smiled. "Sure."

Eve popped another fry into her mouth. "Hey, I've been meaning to ask. What's *really* happening at the salon with Lizbeth?"

I wanted to tell her that I'd been feeling a little strange with Lizbeth there, doing everything so perfectly and never getting anything wrong, but I didn't know *what* to tell her. I didn't want to sound like a mean girl.

"Well, I just feel like . . ."

Before I could say another word, a long, slim form stood next to our table, peering down at us. She wore pristine white jeans and a black blazer with the sleeves cuffed, showing a silk, gray paisley lining. Long, layered silver necklaces hung around her neck, and her chestnut hair was pulled back in a slick ponytail that seemed to tug back the corners of her eyes. My first thought was that she'd fit right in at the salon.

"Hi, girls," the lady said. "I hope I'm not interrupting."

When neither of us said anything at first, she continued to look down at us—at Eve, really, almost like she were inspecting her. Finally I said, "Um, hello?"

She glanced in my general direction, but only for a moment. Then she turned her gaze back to Eve.

"Are you a model?" she asked.

Eve—with her ghostly pale skin—was the one blushing now. "No," she said.

I snorted. I didn't mean to, but that totally sounded like a line. Eve shot me a look, and I hoped she didn't think I was being mean. But seriously, it was a little bit creepy. I decided to be bold. "May we help you?" I asked her.

The lady glanced at me again before turning back to Eve. From nowhere she brandished a thick, white business card, which Eve took from her. "I'm Bunny Jenkins. I've been looking for models all evening." She snapped her fingers and pointed at Eve. "You're perfect. We're casting for a commercial for the new live-action Warpath of Doom game. Heard of it?"

Eve just stared at her, clearly too stunned to speak. "It's a companion to the new alien version of the video game. We're filming a commercial for it next weekend, and your look is perfect for the aliens, just *perfect* with that milky, white skin. If only . . . ," she began.

Eve sat mute, so I said, "What?"

"I was thinking," Bunny said, "that she might look even more stunning if we gave her hair a little kick. Brighten it up a bit, give it some golden highlights to complement the natural paleness. But no." She waved her hand, dismissing the idea. "No time between now and the shoot, just in case it doesn't look right. Maybe just a conditioning treatment. Do you take ballet?"

"I used to do gymnastics," Eve said. She seemed too skinny to catapult herself over a vault, but I guess you would never really know. Looking at my hair, you'd never think I was a hair-styling maven in the making.

"That figures," Bunny said. "Long, lean bodies—very alienlike, if you think about it." She turned to consider me, and I found myself sitting up a bit straighter, readying myself for her inspection. "Too dark and wrong texture of hair. Pretty, but not the right look. Sorry—we're going for naturally pin straight." I felt my back slump back to its natural posture. Just when I'd finally learned to manage my slightly curly hair, it worked me right out of a commercial. Figures. To Eve she said, "What's your name, darling?"

"Eve Benton."

"It's nice to meet you, Eve. I'd love to screen test you if you'll come down to our offices—with your parent or guardian, of course. Google me and my company and you'll see. Okay? Okay," she said, answering her own question. She pointed to her business card, still in Eve's hand. Then she turned on a spiked heel and walked out of the food court.

"Wow," said Eve.

"Seriously," I said. "Are you going to call her?"

"I'm not sure. Should I?"

"Only if you want to be a huge celebrity making millions before your sixteenth," I said.

"I'm not sure," Eve said. "I mean about even wanting to be in a commercial."

"Eve, come on! I bet it'll be so much fun!" I said. "You should do it. Have your mom call Bunny."

Eve looked in the direction Bunny had gone. "She kind of scares me."

"Yeah," I said, also looking in the direction she had gone. I wondered how anyone named Bunny could possibly be intimidating. I thought of her name, and a smile spread across my face. Eve looked at me, and all I had to do was say, "Bunny?" and we started laughing until our stomachs hurt and it was time to head back to Eve's house.

CHAPTER 12

The next day, I was back at the salon, sweeping between Giancarlo's station on the left and Piper's across the aisle on the right. Up front, Lizbeth and Megan stood side by side at reception. Lizbeth wore a red and white striped shirt with a gray skirt, and Megan wore a gray belted shirtdress with black heels. They looked like they'd purposely matched. I wouldn't have been surprised if they had.

I tugged on the ends of my smock, wishing I could look cute, too. At least my hair was looking pretty good, if I did say so. I'd used a new cashmere lather hair product (which is like a soft pomade) to enhance my waves and pulled my long hair into a low side ponytail.

"Mickey," Piper said, breaking into my thoughts. "Could you grab me some extra clips from the back?"

"Sure," I said, and quickly finished up the pile I'd started sweeping.

Today was Piper's turn to do Be Gorgeous. Even though she looked beautiful and amazing in an autumn-orange top that made her strawberry hair pop, she said she was really nervous. "The last time I spoke in front of a crowd was in junior high when I had to give an oral report on the Florida Wetlands. I literally threw up in the bathroom before class."

"Oh, honey, calm down," Giancarlo said. "What's the worst that could happen?"

"I could start babbling nonsense, Chloe would think I'm crazy, and you'd have to drag me out like a crazed maniac?" Piper said.

Giancarlo rolled his eyes. "Picture yourself being fabulous, and fabulosity will follow."

"You make it sound so easy," Piper said.

"It is!"

Devon was nearby listening and said, "Micks. Tell her how you got over being nervous sitting in front of the demo crowd."

I wanted to say, *Under the threat of being fired*, but resisted. "I trusted Devon," I said. Maybe that wasn't 100 percent true—I had been afraid she'd take her revenge on my hair. But later I realized that she took hair way too seriously to give a bad cut, even if she had been upset with me at the time.

Devon nodded in agreement. "Trust yourself," she told Piper. "You *know* you're good."

"Totally!" I said. "I'll help you, whatever you need to keep you calm."

"How about bringing me those clips?"

Once I finally got Piper all the supplies she needed and everything was set for the demo, she went down into the basement to focus, which meant she must have been really desperate for some privacy. That basement was an absolute freak show. I had no proof, but I was pretty sure a colony of rats lived down there, and not like the cute ones from *Ratatouille*. More like oversized zombie rats.

For her demo, Piper was doing what she called messy-classic looks, like jawline pigtails that were ratted out and poufy. As people started to arrive, I showed them to their seats and brought up extra drinks. Mom was at the front greeting them and Megan was running from the front to the back, working on last-minute details. I handed Mom an extra box of pens she'd asked for.

"Thanks, Mickey," Mom said, setting it down and shuffling through some papers at reception. A delivery guy came in with a shipment of new products and Mom showed him to the back.

Lizbeth smiled at me—we hadn't spoken much since we got to work because it'd been so busy. Also she tended to stay in one place and I moved all over the salon. "How was last night?"

I paused—I knew she meant the inventory I'd supposedly been doing with Violet.

I tried to answer without lying—again. "It was okay," I said. "Not so bad." Because hanging out at the mall with Eve wasn't bad at all.

"Did you have to stay late?" Lizbeth asked.

"Nope, not late at all." We'd left the mall around eight thirty.

"That's cool. How long does that take to do, anyway?"

Who was she—a reporter for TMZ?

"Oh, not too long . . . You know!" I finally got the brilliant idea to try to get the heat off me, so I asked, "How was *your* night? What did you and Kristen end up doing?"

"Lizbeth," Mom said, appearing next to us after showing the delivery guy out. "Could you do us a favor?"

"Sure," she said. I let out a subtle sigh of relief. No more questions!

"Could you answer the phones and take any messages that might come in during Piper's demo?" my mom asked Lizbeth. "I want Megan on the floor in case Piper needs anything. I think it'll help calm her down."

Lizbeth's light brown eyes widened. Standing up a little straighter she said, "Yeah, sure!"

"You can just write the appointment requests down here," she said, turning to a fresh page in the notebook that was at reception. "Tell them you'll have Megan call back to confirm. Make sure you get their first and last name and their phone number, even if they tell you we already have it."

"Got it," Lizbeth said. "No problem."

"Hey, Mom," I said. "Um. If you need me to help out on the floor while Piper demos I can do that. Megan can stay here."

Fine, I'll admit it—I was kind of jealous. Mom was letting Lizbeth work the front alone, like a real team member. Lizbeth's star was shooting up quickly while I was still spilling stuff all over the clients. I was practically a liability.

"Thanks, sweetie," Mom said. "But you don't have to worry about this. Lizbeth has things under control up front." She looked over my shoulder. "Besides, it looks like Giancarlo's station needs a sweep." She winked, like she was doing me a favor.

Piper had nothing to worry about. Once she got going with her demo, she was flawless. The girl she used as her model had gorgeous, straight, long blond hair that was versatile enough to be styled two different ways—elegantly swooped to the side, then pulled up in a rockin' ponytail. By the time Piper was done, I was pretty sure I could do the style on myself or someone else. She got tons of cheers, and her beaming smile seemed to say she was happy with how it'd gone. She even did a little curtsy, fanning out her skirt. Afterward I helped clear the chairs away. Soon things were back to the steady buzz of a Saturday.

The front door chimed and Eve walked in with a huge smile on her face.

"Hey, Eve!" Lizbeth said from the front.

"Hi, Lizbeth," she said, standing in front of the reception desk. "Hey, Micks!" she said when she spotted me. Her hair still looked cute from when I'd fixed it last night and touched it up this morning.

"Your hair looks so cute," Lizbeth said.

"All Mickey," Eve said. "But listen!" she turned to me. "You won't believe it! That woman we met last night at the mall? The casting director? My mom checked her out and we went to see her this morning and guess what? I got cast! In the commercial! That's shooting next weekend!"

"Seriously?" I said. The very first thing I thought was that I was excited for Eve. I couldn't believe that someone I knew was going to be on TV. Those thoughts lasted about five seconds, though, because I realized she'd said we'd been at the mall the night before. Together. My heart dropped to the pit of my stomach. Eve didn't know I'd told Lizbeth and Kristen that I'd be slaving away on inventory here at the salon. I decided to just hope Lizbeth hadn't heard that part. "How was the audition? What'd they have you do?" I asked.

"Oh my gosh," Eve began. "They had me stand in these really bright lights and walk really slowly— Bunny said *robotic*. And then they had me throw these blue racquetballs off-camera—like off to the side—*with intense anger*. That's what Bunny said. She told me to pretend they were grenades. Like I know how to handle a grenade! Anyway," she said, taking a breath, "she told me right there on the spot that she liked the way I looked on camera and I was in! Can you believe it?"

"You're amazing, Eve," I said, because I really didn't want to take away from her moment with my own ability to ruin things.

"Wait, back up," Lizbeth said, looking at each of us. I looked down to avoid her gaze. "How did this happen?"

Eve launched into the story of how she was discovered at the food court last night while we were out shopping. The longer her story went on, the more I wondered how I was going to dig myself out of this whopper without ruining my friendships with Lizbeth and Kristen and possibly Eve. Would Eve think I was a liar then, too?

"We were just sitting there, talking about boys—you remember, Mickey?—and she was standing there all tall and slim and model-like. Oh, and get this—her name is Bunny Jenkins. Can you believe it? And she was all, 'Have you ever modeled?' And I was like, 'No,' and she was like, 'You should.'"

All I could do as Eve told her story to Lizbeth was try not to hyperventilate while coming up with some sort of plan to save face over this white lie I had told. Oh, and avoid making eye contact with Lizbeth.

"And then I had the audition and it was just in this one room with lights and a camera, and I had to do the walking and throwing and stuff. And then that was it, and I got it!"

"Wow," Lizbeth said as Eve tried to catch her breath. "That's all kinds of crazy." She looked at me, but only briefly.

"I know, isn't it?" Eve said, still all smiles, all oblivious. "And I'm going to be an alien, but not like a green alien from some lame sci-fi, but like, an albino alien with shiny, almost metallic features. That's what she said, anyway."

"Well, congratulations," Lizbeth said. "That's really an amazing story."

"Thanks," Eve said. "Anyway, I came in because

Bunny said I should get a deep conditioning treatment just to make sure it's at its shiny best. So I guess I'll need an appointment for that."

"You got it. Looks like our first available is next Saturday. Okay?" Lizbeth said.

Eve shrugged. "That's cutting it close, but if that's what you've got, I'll take it!"

Lizbeth wrote down Eve's info.

"Thanks!" she told Lizbeth. "I'll see you guys at school!" Eve ran back outside to her mom's car.

I wanted to bail on the reception area before Lizbeth started asking me questions. I couldn't escape fast enough.

"Hey, Mickey," Lizbeth said. Panic rose up in my throat. "I thought you and Violet were doing inventory here last night?"

Don't lie, a voice inside my head said. *It'll only make it worse.* Then these words came out of my mouth: "Oh, at the last minute Mom said she didn't need me. And, um, I ran into Eve and we just sort of made random plans on the spot."

"So you *didn't* work on Friday?" Lizbeth said. "I thought you told me—"

"Excuse me, Mickey?" Violet said from her station on the other side of Mom's, near the front. "When you get a chance could you bring me some bobby pins from the back?"

"Sure," I said, happy to get away from Lizbeth and her line of questioning. "I better go," I told her.

Lizbeth nodded, but I knew she was suspicious. And more than being mad, she looked hurt at what I'd done—pushing her out of my plans and then lying about it. I didn't like myself for what I'd done, even in the exact moment I was doing it. I knew I'd have to fix it, but once those words had left my mouth, I felt stuck.

For the rest of the day Lizbeth was, I don't know, *professional* toward me or something. Not exactly cold, not exactly friendly, either. I, on the other hand, practically fell all over myself trying to be nice—throwing extra smiles her way and rushing to get her the extra diet sodas we ran out of. None of it seemed to matter, though, because just as she was leaving, I practically yelled good-bye from halfway across the salon. She didn't turn back to say anything.

Maybe she just didn't hear me.

CHAPTER 13

As the school day started on Monday, I dreaded seeing Lizbeth. She had to know I'd lied about the mall; now I just wondered if she'd also told Kristen and, if so, whether or not Kristen hated me, too.

As I walked through the halls I heard little keywords buzzing around the air. Words like *discovered*, *actor*, and *famous*. By lunchtime everyone in our class knew Eve had been cast in a commercial.

"What's this about you shooting a commercial this weekend?" Kristen asked Eve at lunch as she arranged her tray just so. Lizbeth hadn't said a word to me all day, which was basically all the proof I needed that she knew I'd lied.

Eve retold the story. She seemed to enjoy the attention. As she recounted the part about Bunny saying she looked like an alien, I wondered why I hadn't given Eve the heads-up about what I'd told the girls. The last thing I needed was for Eve to dig me further into the mess I'd created by telling our mall story again and again.

Kristen nodded at every detail Eve told, said she loved Bunny's name, and told Eve how lucky she was to have been in the right place at the right time.

"But wait," Kristen said. "When did this happen again?"

I have to say that there was something about the way she asked—and the way she looked through narrowed eyes at Eve—that said she already knew the answer.

"This weekend," Eve said, glancing over at me.

"You guys were together?" she asked, looking straight at me and Eve.

"Yep," Eve said. My heart picked up the pace.

Kristen looked at me and said, "Why didn't *you* get an audition?"

"She didn't want me," I said. "She wanted Eve."

"Right," Kristen said, pulling her tray toward her and stabbing a chicken finger with her spork. "And this was on . . . Saturday night?"

"Kristen," Lizbeth said. "Come on."

"I'm just curious about their weekend," she said in a way that was so overly innocent that it seemed fake. Which meant she knew. She totally knew.

Lizbeth darted her eyes at me before looking down

at her hands. As the silence fell heavier and heavier over our table, Eve said slowly, "Not Saturday. It was Friday."

"Oh, Friday?" Kristen said. She looked at me and continued, "The night you told us you couldn't come over because you had to work? *That* Friday?"

"Kristen, give it a rest," Lizbeth said in a low voice.

"I'm just asking questions."

"Guys, what's going on?" Eve asked.

These gross little nervous sweat bubbles started forming on my upper lip, I could just feel it. *Don't lie,* that voice said. *You'll only get in deeper!* "Okay, so I was supposed to go into the salon on Friday night. It just didn't work out that way so, um, Eve and I just sort of decided to go to the mall." There. The truth, mostly. Except the part about going to Hello, Gorgeous! Friday night in the first place. Eve looked at me, confused about my revised version of events. Thankfully she didn't say anything, though.

"If you had to work, that's cool," Kristen said. "I get it. But if you didn't have to work and you lied, then that's really not cool. If you don't want to hang out with us, you can just say so."

"It's not that at all," I said. I felt awful, but I knew that trying to explain would make matters worse, especially since there was no good explanation. "Look, I'm sorry."

"Do you think they're still doing auditions for the commercial?" Kristen asked Eve.

"I'm pretty sure it's all been cast," Eve said.

Kristen looked down at her lunch. "Figures. I mean, how many times does a commercial shoot in our town? Like, never," she answered. "I feel like I'm being left out of everything."

We all sat stiffly, Eve and I staring wide-eyed and frightened at Kristen's narrowed and angry eyes. Lizbeth didn't look at us when she said, "Hey, K, want to eat outside?"

"Definitely."

As they left, Jonah and Kyle finally made it through the lunch line and plopped down with their trays at the end of the table.

I felt like even Eve was shooting dirty looks at me. There must have been some heavy tension in the air, because once Jonah settled into his lunch, he looked down at us and asked, "What's wrong with you two?"

Instead of explaining what was really going on, I said, "Eve got a part in a commercial. It's shooting this weekend."

"Oh, yeah?" Jonah asked, sticking a spork in his chicken fingers. "If they need a leading man, let me know. I might be able to fit it into my schedule."

"Hilarious," I said.

116

"What's the commercial for?" Kyle asked.

"Oh, just some alien thing," I said, knowing that Jonah was going to flip when he found out. "Something called Warpath of Doom. Heard of it?"

"Dude," Kyle said.

Jonah just about choked on his chicken. "No way."

"For real," Eve said.

"I've been hearing about this place in online forums for months," Jonah said. "It's like the video game, but you get to play inside the game, like in a building. They're calling it The Experience. And then when you play you get to be a character, wearing this sensor vest and carrying a weapon that lasers the targets, and you move through rooms that are the different levels, trying to stay alive to get to the next one. And it's like . . . and you . . . it's only the best . . ." His head shook in little jerks like he couldn't believe what he was hearing. I guess he couldn't. "You're going to be in the commercial for it? That is so *freakin' cool*."

A smile finally cracked Eve's face. "Yeah, I'm pretty excited. We get to go through the game on the shoot. I'll basically be one of the first ones to try it out."

"Whoa," Jonah said, staring at her in awe. "Do you get free passes for when it opens?"

"I don't know," Eve said. "Maybe I'll ask Bunny Jenkins. I guess everyone wants something from this." She muttered that last part, but I was the only one who heard.

"That's so cool," Jonah said, staring at Eve with that familiar look once again—all googly-eyed, like he thought she was the greatest creature in the known universe. Okay, fine—it was actually kind of cute. Still, I could hardly think about anything other than the fact that almost all my friends were mad at me, except maybe Eve. And yeah, I noticed Kyle looking at me throughout the whole convo, but I didn't even care. I was messing everything up with my friends, and that's all that mattered right then.

CHAPTER 14

"Okay, Mick. What was that about?" Eve said as we left the cafeteria.

"It's my fault," I sighed. "Last week, when they asked if I wanted to hang out on Friday night, I lied. I told them I had to work."

"Why would you do that?"

"I didn't want to invite them to the mall since you said it should be just us, and I didn't want them to be mad that we were doing something without them," I said and shrugged. It sounded so lame.

"Well, they're mad now," Eve said. "You could have just said you had plans and left it at that. Then you wouldn't have been lying, and you wouldn't have hurt their feelings, either."

"Believe me," I said. "I know that now."

"Mickey, you have to fix it," Eve said.

I knew she was right. I just had no idea how.

"For the most part, great job on these reports," Ms. Carter said from the front of the Little Theater the next afternoon as she held up a stack of papers.

I wondered who she was talking about when she'd said *for the most part*. Was she aiming her laser eyes at me? Sure, I'd struggled a bit to write the required five pages, but I was pretty sure I'd pulled it off in the end. Hopefully.

I sat beside Eve. Kristen and Lizbeth sat two rows behind us. I'd saved them seats and tried to wave them over when they came in a bit late, but they hadn't seen me. I think. It's also possible that they completely and purposely ignored me.

When Jonah arrived with Kyle, he moved my bags from the seats and plopped down. "Thanks for saving," he'd said, and I didn't correct him.

"Before we hand back your papers, we have a special speaker today," Ms. Carter announced. "Joyce Clemens is from the human resources department of Briggs & Meyers. Now, when you go in for a job interview . . ."

"You have to say something to Lizbeth and Kristen," Eve whispered to me. "I think they're really mad."

"I know," I said out of the corner of my mouth. The other teachers were keeping an eye out. "But I said I was sorry yesterday."

She shook her head. "Not really."

She was right. I had said I was sorry, but I hadn't explained what I was sorry for. Plus I, um, sort of lied again. So . . . yeah. I definitely had more work to do.

"Everyone, let's thank Miss Clemens for speaking to us today," Ms. Carter said a little while later. We applauded. I had learned nothing since I was way too busy thinking about my *current* life and not some fantasy life in which I wore a suit to some job interview.

"Line up by last name to receive your written reports. Zs up front. And keep the noise down, please," Ms. Carter said. Of course, we immediately erupted into chatter.

We all got up from our rows and shuffled to the front. I heard Kristen behind us in the crowd squealing.

"Oh my god, Lizbeth!" Kristen said. "Did you hear that? Saturday tennis and barbeque!"

"I wonder what that's about?" Eve asked, looking over her shoulder at them.

"Probably something at the country club," I said.

"Mickey Wilson," Ms. Carter said when she spotted me, two from the stage. She held my paper out to me— all five pages, stapled together with a big, red grade on the front that I couldn't see. "I expected much more from you, young lady."

I took the paper from her as a feeling of disbelief

washed over me. There was a big, red C at the top. How could that be? "Did you honestly think I wouldn't notice enlarged fonts and shrunken margins?" she said. I stared back blankly. "Did you even bother to spell-check this?"

"I spell-checked," I said, even though I wasn't totally sure I had.

"And despite Hello, Gorgeous! being a beauty salon, I don't think it's only about knowing how to look glamorous. Do you?"

"No."

"And from what I understand, your mother started this business from scratch. I would have liked to have read about that, and perhaps how it affected your family. Something from an insider's perspective." She sighed and said, "I certainly expect more from you on your oral report or your overall grade will suffer." I stood staring at my paper—I'd never have thought I'd get graded this low on anything to do with hair. "This paper must be signed by your mother and brought back to me. Okay?"

I felt myself nodding, unable to believe it. My mother was going to kill me. And possibly bar me from Hello, Gorgeous! My salon dreams were over, finished, never gonna happen.

Somehow I made my way to the exit doors of the Little Theater.

"Hey," Eve said. "How'd you do?"

"I'm toast," I said. "Eve, I got a C. For working at my own mother's salon! A place where I've spent practically my entire life!"

"Ouch! But I'm sure it's not that bad. You can make it up with your next report," she said.

"You don't understand," I said. "My mom always said that if I didn't keep up my grades she wouldn't let me work there. And getting *this* grade on *this* paper is, like, a major red flag."

We walked down the halls to lunch together. Kristen and Lizbeth were ahead of us—clearly not waiting for me and Eve. I wondered what grade Lizbeth had gotten on her paper, figuring it was probably better than what I had gotten.

Maybe the teachers had just graded hard this time? I could use that as an excuse when I showed my mom.

"Hey, so what'd you get?" I asked Eve.

Eve looked a little guilty when she said, "An A."

I knew that Eve deserved her good grade, but I still felt a slight (growing into huge) panic about my C.

Inside the caf, Eve and I started toward our regular table. Just as we sat down, I turned to see Kristen and Lizbeth walking right past us.

"Uh-oh," I said.

Eve looked. "We'll do this together," she told me. "Kristen! You guys, come sit with us!"

They looked back at us, hesitating. "You sure you want us to? You sure you don't want some alone time?" Kristen asked, sharing a meaningful look with Lizbeth.

"Come on, don't be like that," Eve said.

"We're not being like anything, Eve," Kristen said. My stomach tightened. This wasn't going to be easy. Kristen looked around the caf as if searching for a better option. I guess she didn't find one because she said, "Fine."

When we were all seated at the table, Eve gave my arm a nudge. I took a deep breath.

"You guys, look," I said. Kristen's mouth was shut tight; Lizbeth, though, kept her eyes on me like she was eager to hear what I had to say. "I'm really sorry about Friday night. Honestly. I know you're mad, but we didn't mean to leave you out of our plans. And I'm the one who lied, not Eve, so don't be mad at her."

"But really," Eve said. "It wasn't a big deal, us going to the mall. We should all do something again soon, though. Like maybe this weekend?"

"Are you sure you don't have to do more inventory or something?" Kristen said. Lizbeth stared me down, not missing a single word I said or gesture or look I made. She made me so uncomfortable that I could barely look at her. "I just want to make sure Lizbeth and I don't get in your way or anything."

"Kristen . . . ," Eve began.

Kristen unpacked her lunch, looking like she was going to devour it—and not because she was hungry. No one said anything for about five years.

"Seriously, though," Eve said, picking the conversation back up. "We could have another sleepover. This weekend or whenever you guys want."

"Can't," Kristen said, biting into an orange slice. "We've already got weekend plans. Barbeque and tennis tournament at the country club. *With the boys.*"

If I didn't know better, I'd think she was trying to get back at us. Actually, I was still trying to figure Kristen out, so maybe she was. As if I'd be jealous of them going to their schmancy country club with some stupid boys.

"Maybe some other time," Lizbeth said—to Eve. It was like she made a point of not looking at me when she said it. You know—*to Eve?*

"Oh, cool," Eve said, keeping her upbeat attitude. I couldn't think of anything to say that didn't involve groveling, so I was useless. Then Eve said, "So, Mickey! Tell us who's doing Be Gorgeous this weekend."

I took Eve's cue to move on from the subject of weekend plans and help her out with the small talk.

We had apologized to them and tried to explain. What else could we do?

"This weekend it's a good one," I said, "Giancarlo is doing it."

"I bet that's going to be amazing," Eve said. "Kristen, I bet his hairstyles will be right up your style alley. I've only met him once, but he seems like he's really edgy when it comes to hair. Wait," Eve said. "He'll still be able to do my hair, right? I'm coming in on Saturday for my commercial on Sunday."

"Of course."

Um, that was Lizbeth speaking. Not me. You know, *me*, the one whose mom runs the salon? And who came up with the idea of Be Gorgeous?

"We've got you booked for the deep conditioning right after his Be Gorgeous session. No problem."

Yeah. That was Lizbeth again.

"So," I said to Lizbeth. "Since there's that barbeque-tennis thing at the club on Saturday, are you taking part of the day off or something?"

"Why would I take part of the day off?" Lizbeth said as if it were the most ridiculous question in the world.

"To hang out with the guy you've been drooling over half the year? And because I was just guessing that the tournament will happen during the day," I said.

Lizbeth blushed and looked around as if Matthew might have heard from two tables down. "I have not been *drooling* over him, Mickey. And I'd never take a Be Gorgeous day off work. It's only the most important day of the week, and my last day working at the salon."

Did Kristen just—yeah, she did. She totally just rolled her eyes at Lizbeth's dedication to Hello, Gorgeous! Maybe she actually wanted Lizbeth to skip work to hang out with her and the boys?

"It's not like the whole place will fall apart if you're not there," I said. I felt like she was making a point of showing what a great employee she was by not taking a day off. "We have Megan. And you could make it up on Sunday."

"That's okay. I'm not about to miss my last official Saturday. Besides, I can go to the barbeque after my shift."

"True," I said, trying to act cool. But what had she meant by last "official" Saturday? Did she plan on working some unofficial days as well? Like, start working there for real even after Career Ex was over? A sweat broke out on my upper lip. "I'm just saying, if you want to go hang out at the club, I'm sure it's no big deal."

"It's a big deal to me, missing work. I told your mom I'd work there all through Career Ex and not take any shortcuts. So I'll stay for the whole day, thanks."

After that everyone got kind of quiet and stayed that way. Eve didn't try to start any more light conversations, Kristen didn't lash out at anyone, and Lizbeth didn't snap at me. The silence was deafening. I looked at my three friends and marveled at the wreckage I'd created so effortlessly.

Nice job, Mickey.

＊＊＊

That night, I sat at my vanity practicing my mom's signature. She signed her name in a tall, slim script that I was determined to perfect. Still, no matter how hard I tried, mine looked too bubbly. It was hopeless. Oh yeah, and wrong. I was pretty sure that forging an adult's signature was illegal, even if it was just for some dumb school report.

I finally summoned my nerve and marched downstairs, paper in hand. Mom and Dad were curled up on the couch watching some documentary about one of those old wars. It looked insanely boring. But, um, educational. I thought maybe I should let them watch it and bother Mom with that pesky little signature later. Better yet, I could show them how interested I was in educational stuff and sit with them. That way when they saw my grade I could be all, *Yeah, I'm really trying to learn more about the world and stuff.*

"Can I watch with you guys?" I asked. It couldn't

hurt to put the whole grade thing off for a few minutes—or hours, which was how long these docs seemed to last.

"Sure, honey," Dad said, adjusting to make room for me.

"Wait a second," Mom said, not budging. She knew already, and it wasn't fair. You couldn't get anything past her. "You're interested in the War of 1812? What've you got there?" She nodded to the crumpled up paper in my hand.

"Oh this?" I waved the paper. "Nothing. Just this report I had to write for school."

"Is that the one for your Career Exploration class?" Mom asked, and I nodded. "Lizbeth told me about it— she actually interviewed me for it." *Great,* I thought. Perfect Lizbeth. This should make my terrible grade seem that much worse. "How'd you do?"

"Oh, well, um, not too bad."

"Mickey already knows everything about the salon," Dad said. "Of course she did great!"

Mom held out her hand for the paper. Reluctantly, I handed it to her along with a black pen. "Could you sign it?"

She took the paper, unrolled it and started to sign until she saw the grade. That fat, round letter C. "What is this? A C? This is the report you did for the class with Lizbeth?"

I wished she wouldn't keep bringing up Lizbeth. I also wished I'd thought of interviewing Mom myself.

"Yes," I said.

"Mikaela, what have I told you about working at the salon and your grades?"

"What'd she get?" Dad asked, looking over Mom's shoulder. When he saw the grade he actually cringed and said, "Oh, Mickey." He crushed me.

Mom didn't take her eyes off me when she said, "How could you have done so poorly on an assignment that was practically tailor-made for you?"

I looked down at the antique rug beneath my feet. "I don't know."

"Lizbeth has been doing such a great job that I thought that if all was fine with her, then I certainly didn't have to worry about you. I guess I was wrong," she sighed. "You know, Mickey, you could learn a thing or two from Lizbeth. She's a sharp girl."

I couldn't believe she'd just said that. "Yeah, she's sharp all right," I said, rolling my eyes.

Mom eyed me and said, "Watch it." I looked back down at the rug, not wanting to get myself in worse trouble. Mom signed the paper and held it out to me. "Lizbeth said you also have to do an oral report?" I nodded, wondering how much she and Lizbeth had talked about. "I suggest you put some effort into that. A lot. If your grades slip I'll have no choice but to—"

"Mom, I know."

"Watch your tone," she said. "I suggest you do a better job on your final report. Do you understand me?"

"Yes," I said.

Upstairs in my room I wondered if there'd ever be a week when I wouldn't worry about disappointing my mom or losing my job. Maybe for a little while things could be cool. Maybe for one day Mom could be as proud of me as she seemed to be of Lizbeth.

CHAPTER 15

Before Saturday at the salon rolled around, I had to know just how great Lizbeth's masterpiece, otherwise known as her written report, was. Since she was still being steely toward me, I had Eve find out. Should I have been surprised that she got an A on it? Of course not. She was perfect at the salon. I should have been surprised that she didn't get an A-plus-plus-plus on it. I had to get over it, though, and work on making her not hate me. I told myself I shouldn't be jealous of her grade and that she had a right to still be a little upset with me.

By the time I got to the salon on Saturday, I swore to myself that I'd for real, no joking around, stop being so jealous of Lizbeth and start being extra nice to her. Particularly while we were still working together.

"I love those metallic bracelets," I told her of the silver, gold, and copper bracelets clinking on her wrist. She was straightening up the drinks area, preparing for the styling session. "The clients mostly drink diets. I always stock extra so I won't run out," I said lamely.

"I got it," she said, pointing beneath the table to the small cooler I'd never seen. It was packed with ice and more diet sodas.

"Oh," I said. I guess she was more prepared than I gave her credit for. Clearly she didn't need my help. "Where'd you get that cooler?"

"Down in the basement," she said. She didn't look at me. "There's a ton of stuff down there no one ever uses. Someone should really clean it up."

I wanted to say that *someone* would never be me—Hello! Zombie rats!—but instead I said, "Sounds like a good project for a slow day."

She kept straightening the station even though it was perfect.

"Are you going to leave early so you can go to the tennis tournament thing?"

She shook her head. "No. I told you—I don't want to flake out on the busiest day of the week. Especially since Giancarlo is styling today." She shot her eyes at me for a flash of a moment. "Why do you keep asking me?"

"I don't," I said. Had I been? Maybe I felt like she might give up work for a little fun like I had done when I had my sleepover. Was that such an awful thing to do? "I just don't want you to miss out on a fun time with Kristen and the boys, that's all."

"I like being here. And I can do both. I told you."

Before I could say "Yes, I *know* you told me," Mom appeared behind us, looking sleek and polished in a white, tailored suit.

"Everybody getting ready?" Mom asked. "Lizbeth, it looks great up here, as usual. What's this?" She tapped the cooler with her bone patent-leather peep toe.

"Extra diets," Lizbeth said. "Actually, I should move it out of sight." She picked up the cooler and put it beneath the reception desk.

"Lizbeth, you are reading my mind," Mom said. I wanted to say something about how *perfect* Lizbeth was, but I kept my mouth shut. No more snark from me.

Giancarlo's session was the best yet. His model had long, thin hair and he showed how to give it height and volume, then did it up in a messy ballerina bun. He finished off the session with long, relaxed, easy curls.

While Giancarlo worked his magic, I kept to my standard duties (minus the drinks station) but stayed out of the way of the demo, sweeping silently around the other stylists. I watched from the back as Lizbeth worked the reception area basically on her own. Mom sent Megan on an emergency run to the bank and I guess she asked Lizbeth to cover again. She answered the phones and greeted clients in a lowered voice so she wouldn't disturb Giancarlo's demo (as if his booming voice could possibly be overshadowed).

"Great job, everyone," Mom said once the chairs had been cleared away. Giancarlo was swarmed by women asking questions and requesting appointments. There were always lots of parties at this time of year, and the women wanted him to style them for all their events.

I swept a little pile near reception, and after I dumped my pan, Mom was back there talking to Lizbeth.

". . . maybe on Sunday. What do you think?" Mom was saying.

"Wow, thanks, Chloe," Lizbeth said. "I'll have to check with my mom, but I think I'd, like, really like that."

I accidentally-on-purpose kicked the trash can slightly, making just enough racket for them to see me.

"Oh, Mickey," Mom said. "Good job today. I was just talking to Lizbeth—she offered to start clearing out the basement tomorrow. So what do you think? Want to help her?"

"But I *work* on Sundays," I said. "Alone."

"I'm aware. You also have a big assignment to prepare for, don't you?" Mom said. "You should probably be concentrating on that instead of what days you work." Lizbeth at least had the decency to look embarrassed as Mom practically scolded me. "I know the oral report for Career Exploration is coming up. Maybe you two could work on something together? Like a team project? You could certainly use the help after your last grade." Mom shook her head at the memory of that horrible C.

Truly, I couldn't believe it. My own mother was playing favorites to a friend of mine—the *real* salon wizard in the making.

"I can do it on my own," I said. "I don't need any help."

"Are you sure about that?" Mom asked.

I almost snapped back that I was 100 percent sure, thanks *so* very much, but just then the door chimed and Eve walked in.

"Hi, Eve!" Lizbeth said. Cheered is more like it. I guess she'd forgiven Eve for going to the mall without her.

"Hi, Eve!" I echoed, like I was letting Lizbeth know that Eve was my friend, too. She was my friend first if we had to get technical about it.

"I'll leave you to it," Mom said to Lizbeth. "But

let's talk more about tomorrow, okay?"

"Thanks, Chloe," Lizbeth said.

"Thank *you*. I've really appreciated your easy manner here on these three Saturdays when it was so chaotic." Then, I swear, she looked at me, like I was the one who caused all the chaos.

That was it.

As Mom walked back to her office, a new level of frustration rose inside me. I had to show her. I had to prove to her that I was as worthy a member of the salon team as Lizbeth was. And not just as the sweeper and occasional gofer, fetching pins and clips and sterilized combs for the stylists. I was good at a lot of things, and someday I'd be the best stylist at the salon. Maybe even better than my own mother. I just had to prove myself.

Lizbeth was good at taking down names and phone numbers and greeting people as they came in, but I'd never heard her say she wanted this, like for a real job. I'd never seen her drool over new hair accessories the way I did on a regular basis. She never talked about the fishtail braid as if it were the most revolutionary thing since the invention of the flat iron. I'm not saying she didn't want it; I'm just saying she didn't show it. And if you loved something as much as I loved this world of beauty, how could you *not* show it?

"I hope you don't mind waiting a bit," Lizbeth said to Eve. "Giancarlo is a little backed up from his demo. It was a raging success, but what'd you expect?" Lizbeth smiled, but I noticed Eve looked a bit panicked.

"Everything okay?" I asked her.

"I'm kind of in a rush," she said.

Lizbeth looked at the schedule and said, "You're just in for a deep conditioning, right?"

"Yes," Eve said, "but I have a fitting with the wardrobe people in an hour and I can't be late. Bunny said there would be consequences if anyone was." She looked extremely petrified at this possibility. "How far behind is he?"

Lizbeth looked at the schedule, then looked back at Giancarlo laughing it up with a group of ladies. He didn't look like he was in any sort of rush.

"Once he gets you all washed and applies the conditioner, you're supposed to sit under the dryer for at least half an hour," Lizbeth told her. When Eve started cracking her fingers, I could tell she was nervous. That Bunny must have been some piece of work.

"Wait here," I told Eve. "Let me go see what *I* can do."

Eve turned her frightened eyes on me and said, "Thanks, Mickey. You're a lifesaver."

As I walked away I heard Lizbeth say to her, "Don't worry, Eve. We'll take care of it."

We? Try me.

I broke into Giancarlo's conversation as delicately as I could. "Um, excuse me. Giancarlo? Your next client is here. You about ready for her?"

But I should have known better. When Giancarlo is the center of attention, there's no pulling him away.

"Have you ladies met the amazing Mickey?" he asked, completely ignoring my question. "She is a styling queen!" For once I didn't want the attention, since I was feeling a little ragged. "This girl has such amazing style that she'll have her own beauty empire before she gets to high school."

Oh, that flatterer, Giancarlo—I was pretty sure he didn't mean half of what he said. Besides, even though I liked hearing I was brilliant, I had to keep him on task. "Giancarlo, your three o'clock is here. My friend Eve? When do you think you'll be able to see her? She's kind of in a rush."

"Okay, okay, I hear you," he said.

"Should I see if one of the other stylists can take her? Since she's not getting it cut or anything, just a deep conditioning?" I asked, thinking what a good problem solver I was.

He suddenly stopped and put his hand up on

his expansive hip. "Give away my client? I don't think so."

"It's just that she's in a hurry," I said.

"Oh, everyone's in a hurry." He looked back at the woman in his chair and continued giving style tips. When they started talking about different highlights for spring and fall, I groaned.

I knew there was no way Eve could wait for him—or more to the point, Bunny couldn't wait for Eve. Now was my chance to remind everyone that I was capable of amazing things.

If there was one thing I'd learned from reading about legendary stylists, it was that if you wanted to be great, you had to take major risks. I was ready to plunge headfirst into greatness.

I walked back up to the front where Eve and Lizbeth were talking.

"I didn't see it," Lizbeth was saying. "But maybe Kristen found it after we left."

"I'm pretty sure I lost it on the couch last night when we were watching the movie," Eve said. "It probably fell into the cushions."

"When I see Kristen later today, I'll tell her to look there."

"Thanks," Eve said. "Mickey! What'd he say?" she asked, just seeing me.

I leaned on the counter and tried not to wonder

what they'd been talking about. But what *had* they been talking about? Had they all been hanging out without me?

"Giancarlo is just a bit behind schedule," I said.

"Oh, great," Eve said, her shoulders sinking.

"But I have an idea," I said. I had to focus on my idea, which wasn't just good. It was foolproof. "I can help you if you want me to. *I* can give you the conditioning treatment. It's easy, and I've seen the stylists do it a thousand times. Really, there's nothing to it."

Eve looked at me at bit skeptically. She checked the clock on the wall and said, "I don't know . . ."

Lizbeth looked like she was working out a way to be the hero herself. But I needed Mom and everyone else to know that I was still a styling wonder. "I promise, the treatment is a piece of cake. It'll be fine."

"Well I don't want to be late for my fitting. Bunny might go into a psychotic rage or something." She took a deep breath. "Okay. Let's do it."

"Great! Just follow me to the back," I said.

Lizbeth had a look on her face that said more than I wanted to hear as we walked away. Maybe she was still mad at me about the mall thing. Maybe she was still so mad she'd tell my mom on me. If Mom found out what I was about to do, she'd never see what a legit stylist I was. I had to make sure Lizbeth didn't blow it for me.

"Just go back by the changing room," I told Eve. "I'll be there in two secs." I went back to reception and said to Lizbeth, "Hey!" As if we hadn't just seen each other three-point-two seconds ago. "So, like, if anyone comes looking for me or Eve, it's okay. I mean, we'll be right back. No biggie." Why couldn't I think of something on the fly?

"What are you talking about?" Lizbeth asked, her brow all crinkled.

"Oh! Ha!" I almost slapped my forehead, then realized it'd look bogus and stopped my hand midair as if I were about to bless her. "What I mean is, Eve and I are going to the back to . . . look at the . . . um. The mineral deposits!" Lizbeth stared at me like I'd just told her I was quitting school to be a full-time plumber. "Don't you have that in science class? That section on mineral deposits?"

She slowly shook her head. "No."

"Well we do and it's, like, really important to our teacher that we learn about them. Supposedly they can be found in rusty sinks and stuff." (Quick aside: I had zero idea what I was talking about.) "*Anyway*," I said as if this were all irrelevant. "Just, if anyone is looking for us, tell them we're busy. But don't tell them where we are. Mom will get mad if she knows I'm doing schoolwork at the salon."

That was a real whopper, since Mom would never do

or say anything to discourage me from doing school stuff. But I guess I'd thrown Lizbeth far enough off course because she said "whatever" and went back to answering phones. Only then was I able to head back to Eve and finally make a name for myself.

CHAPTER 16

"Um, where are we going?" Eve asked when I opened the door that led to the basement.

"Right down here." I pulled the door shut behind me. The light above the stairs was a single bulb on a string, shining dimly down the metal staircase. Someone had left the light on below, although it wasn't exactly the warm, sunshiny light that shone inside the salon. It seemed gray and unsteady, like an old black-and-white movie. Of a hospital room. During a war. Just after it was bombed.

It didn't exactly inspire me, but if I could create beauty down here, I could create it anywhere.

"Come on," I said. "Right this way."

"Um, why are we going down here?" Eve asked, her footsteps slowly following me.

"It'll give us more space," I improvised. "And

privacy. It's so crazy upstairs, don't you think? Much calmer down here."

"More like abandoned. And eerie. And downright creepy. Mickey?"

"Yeah?"

"Seriously."

Eve stopped on the bottom step. I looked around at the scene in the basement. It was your regular beauty shop graveyard. Old hard-hat hair dryers, plastic boxes full of busted curling and flat irons, cases full of dusty hair products that never sold. Lizbeth was right—someone really needed to clean the place up.

I checked the plug for one of the hard-hat dryers; after a moment of sputtering, it cranked to life.

"Ha! It works!" I said, looking at Eve. Her eyes scanned the floor, probably looking out for roaches and rats. I pulled an old chair out from against the wall—an orange plastic seat with a metal-bar back that I remembered from when I was a kid. Its familiarity calmed me. I patted the seat. "Step right up!"

Eve walked tentatively to the chair. "Are you sure you can see down here? It's pretty dark. And there's no mirror."

"It's fine! Don't worry! Let's just get you a robe." I looked around the boxes, bursting apart with more dusty products and an old washer and dryer that hadn't worked for years. I'd have to run upstairs to get her a robe. Then I had another idea. There was more on the line here than just showing Mom. I also had to figure out how to make a splash with my oral report. If I did some really unbelievably amazing thing here, and talked about it for the report . . . "Okay, Eve. Here's what I'm thinking." *Blow them away*, that's what I was thinking. "You need something more than just a boring old conditioning treatment, right? Something to really help brighten your hair up, especially for such a big-deal occasion. So I'm thinking . . ."

Eve raised a brow at me. "Yeah?"

"I'm thinking just the tiniest bit of color will make all the difference. It'll give you that *wow*, that *pow* you need to really stand out on the set tomorrow."

"Color?" Eve asked. "I don't know, Mickey. Bunny said she didn't want to risk coloring my hair so close to filming."

I felt like one of those screaming salespeople you see on Saturday afternoon TV—except for the screaming part. I would sell this to her, even if she thought she didn't want it. "Don't you really want to impress her? This'll just enhance what you've got naturally. Plus, the dye has moisturizers in it, so it'll be like getting a deep conditioning, anyway. It's like a two in one!"

Eve looked at me, then down at the chair—kind

of as if it were the electric kind, if you know what I mean. Finally she said, "I don't know. Are you sure there's even time?"

"Totally sure! I'll just do some well-placed highlights. It won't take any time at all. Let me just run upstairs and get some supplies," I said, dashing up the staircase before she flat-out said no.

Like a supersleuth, I snagged a robe, then went into the supply room where we kept the hair dyes. Piper came in and I acted very interested in straightening the tubes of dye and the little plastic bowls in which the stylists mix the colors. When she left I grabbed two tubes, glancing at the color shades. I got a bowl and a brush, and on my way out I took a stack of foil squares used to section the hair and paint on the color. I was set.

In the basement I channeled the other stylists as I squeezed the two tubes into the bowl and stirred them with the brush. They always chatted up their clients to get them to relax. And to get the latest gossip!

"So," I said as I stirred the dye in the bowl. "What'd you leave at Kristen's?" Ugh, I could never be smooth about anything. You'd think I could have asked her how she was liking the weather or something first instead of slamming into the big question I was dying to know about.

"My bracelet," she said. "I totally wish you'd been there. It felt weird without you."

I couldn't believe it. Was it possible that Kristen was still so mad about my mall trip with Eve that she non-vited me to her house? I thought that was so over.

I said to Eve, "This was last night?" I looked at the color the dye was turning from mixing the two. In the light it looked a little dark, but I couldn't be sure. Mostly all I could see was my three friends having fun without me.

"Yeah," Eve said. "When you were having your dinner or whatever with your parents."

Oh, come on. "I wasn't having dinner," I said, really beating the dye now. "I wasn't invited to Kristen's house." I was angry, but also sad. Why was Kristen getting back at me like this?

"Wait, seriously?" she asked, turning a bit to look at me. "Well, I mean . . . I'm sure it was a mix-up or something . . . ," she said, but didn't sound convinced. She looked up at me with big, watery eyes, like just the thought of Kristen purposely not inviting me could send her to tears. "Mickey, it's . . ." She sniffed and rubbed her eyes. "Sorry, but that dye is pretty strong, isn't it? It's burning my eyes." She rubbed her eyes with the heels of her hands.

I looked at the color in the bowl, which was now a

milky white, nice and crisp. The smell didn't bother me, but maybe I was used to it from working at the salon? Anyway, I had to refocus and concentrate on right now, not last night.

"It's normal. And, uh, the smell will fade." Totally made that up. "Can you hold these?" I asked, handing her the stack of foils.

"Sure," she said, sniffing once more.

When she saw the bowl of dye she sucked in her breath.

"Oh, this?" I said, gesturing to it with the brush. "Don't worry, the color looks different here than it will on your head. The chemicals work with, uh, your hair follicles, see? And the reaction makes it change colors. It's actually really cool." I gotta be honest—I was pretty proud of myself for sounding so official.

"So what color *is* my hair going to be?" Eve asked.

"It's really going to shine, just like Bunny said." Which I knew didn't exactly answer the question, but I needed less convo and more concentration.

I started to feel tiny, little sweat bubbles springing on my upper lip. I wiped them away with the back of my hand, then snapped on the protective gloves I'd gotten from upstairs. They were a bit big, and I hoped they didn't make working more difficult. I moved on, sectioning off the first bit of her hair.

"I'm either the world's best friend," Eve said, "or

the world's dumbest person to let you do this."

"Foil," I said, holding out my clear-gloved hand. Eve passed a shiny square to me. Working the pointed tip of the brush to get that one little section wasn't as quick and easy-looking as the stylists make it look. "I can see it all perfectly in my mind. Gorgeous!" I laid the section of hair across the foil. "Um, could you hold this, too?" I asked, handing her the dye. I tugged up my gloves, which were slipping, then dipped my brush in the dye bowl. It didn't look like enough, so I really scooped some color on it, then brushed it on Eve's hair, making sure to get it really close to the scalp to cover the roots. Once I'd totally covered the section, I held the brush handle in my teeth, then folded the foil into a small, if uneven, square. I pressed it tightly to her head.

"It's kind of tight," Eve said, pushing her fingers on the foil.

"Um, it's supposed to be," I said, even though I wasn't exactly sure.

I started on the next section, accidentally brushing the color on my forearm above the glove as I tried to cover the whole section of long hair. I told myself that it was all going to be worth it when Mom saw what an amazing job I'd done. She'd be stunned at my technique, and I could just hear Violet and Giancarlo praising me on my incredible skills. Lizbeth would beg me to dye her hair next. By this time next year, Mom might even give me my own chair with my own clients. I'd be styling all the girls in school, and hosting my own Be Gorgeous demo!

"Um, Mickey?" Eve said. "It's kind of starting to burn."

"Burn?"

"Yeah. *Burn*. On my scalp."

My heart started to beat faster, and sweat continued to form on my lip. "Are you sure?"

"*Yes,* I'm sure. It's burning really bad. And I should let you know that I didn't cry when I broke my leg in second grade, so I can take pain. But this is *bad*."

I'd only done maybe half her hair, one side and halfway around the back. And, actually, now that she'd mentioned the burning, my forearm, where I'd smeared a little of the coloring, was starting to tingle ever so slightly. I knew from being around the salon all these years that everyone reacted to color differently. I'd just never heard of dye making a client's scalp burn.

"Mickey," she said, her voice shaking this time. "It really burns."

I looked and saw that her eyes were watering. "Okay, no problem. I'm pretty sure I've heard other stylists say it gets a little like this."

"Pretty sure?"

"Let's just, um . . ."

"Wash it out!" she cried. "Get it out of my hair!"

With visions of Eve's hair falling out in chunks, I raced her over to the sink. I started taking the foils out, and she grabbed at them, too, practically yanking them out.

"Put your head under here," I said, trying to keep the panic out of my voice.

"Hurry!" she said, tossing off another foil. There were no salon sink chairs in the basement, so Eve had to lean awkwardly over the ledge, sticking her head under the faucet.

When I turned it on, it clanked . . . then clanged . . . then sputtered some brown liquid . . . then moaned and quit altogether.

"Oh, shoot."

"Mickey, please!"

"Come on," I said to the sink, willing it to work. I tried the hot water faucet, and it sputtered as well, but after a few kicks, it came to life. I stuck my hand under the faucet—it felt slightly warm but not too bad. "Back under, Eve." She put her head in the stream of lukewarm water as I washed the dye out with my hands. "How does it feel?" I asked, trying to ignore the water that ran blue-gray. Probably just the bad lighting.

"Still burns!" she shouted.

"What is going on down here?"

I froze with my hand on Eve's head, keeping it under the heavy flow of water.

"Oh my gosh," I said, looking up to see my mother standing on the stairs, taking in the scene I'd created with a look of complete disbelief.

"Mickey?" Eve yelled over the running water. "I'm telling you, Mickey, I can't take it! It's *still* burning!"

Mom crossed the basement toward us as Eve finally pushed my hand away and stood up from the sink, grabbing the towel I had set on top of a box. She was on the verge of crying, her eyes red and watery. She took a section of her hair from the front side and looked down at it.

"Oh my gosh," she slowly said. She looked up and saw my mom standing before her, and in her shock Eve asked Mom, "What is this? What did she do to my hair?"

"It's okay, honey," Mom said, taking Eve by the shoulders. "Hurry now, let's get you upstairs."

"What did she do?" Eve mumbled like an insane person as Mom gently led her away. "What did I let her do?"

Mom guided her up the steps, patting her back as Eve kept walking. Mom stopped and looked back down at me, the soft, concerned look she'd had for Eve completely gone. Through gritted teeth, she pointed her finger at me and said, "Go home right this minute."

It was like I could feel her surge of anger crushing me. I couldn't even speak. Mom turned away from me—angry, disgusted, probably both—and stomped back upstairs.

I somehow made it out of the basement. Mom didn't even look at me as I passed by the sinks where she was with Eve, even though I know she must have seen me. As she began rinsing Eve's hair, Eve's shaky voice asked Mom, "Do you think I'll still be able to make it to my fitting?"

"I don't know, sweetie," Mom said. "We better call your mom first."

As I walked toward the front door, I could feel everyone looking at me. Giancarlo had his hand on his hip, looking between me and Eve. Devon continued working on her client, but her eyes darted up to look at me as if I'd stolen her tips. Just about everyone stared as I did my walk of shame—everyone except Lizbeth. Like Mom, she wouldn't even look at me.

I knew she and Kristen were still mad about the mall, and that they'd purposely made plans without me last night for revenge or something. So maybe I hadn't exactly been the greatest friend lately, but I never thought Lizbeth would do this to me. How could she have ratted me out?

CHAPTER 17

When I tried the front door at home, I realized I'd left my bag at the salon along with my house key, and naturally Dad wasn't there to let me in. I knew the back door would be locked but I checked it, anyway, and, yep, I was completely shut out.

I sat on one of the chaise lounge chairs on our back porch and stared aimlessly at the sky, wishing I could turn my brain off and not think about what had just happened. This wasn't a couple of nail polishes I'd taken without permission—this was big. I knew without a doubt that this was the end of my salon days. No way would Mom let me keep working there after this. Why would she? I wouldn't if I were her.

What if Eve's hair fell out? Images of her with a bald head kept running through my mind. I wondered what Mom was going to do to me, and if she could save Eve's hair.

I couldn't believe Lizbeth would do this to me. What a rat. It was like she and Kristen had managed a double assault by not inviting me out on Friday, then busting me at work on Saturday.

I sat up on the chair, realizing I was still wearing my lowly smock. I took it off, then crossed the yard and headed over to Jonah's house. I didn't feel like talking to anyone, but I also knew I needed someone to talk to. And in all my worry I'd somehow forgotten that Jonah's parents hold on to our extra house key. That would be useful just now.

I knocked twice on Jonah's back door and then let myself in.

"Hello?" I called.

"Hey!" I heard Jonah call from the direction of his room. "In here!"

Thankfully he wasn't playing Warpath. I wasn't in the mood to see the video game Eve was supposed to be in a commercial for—that is, until I came along and ruined everything, including her hair. *Especially* her hair.

"Hi," I said, almost tripping on some skateboard wheels he'd left by the door.

"Hey," he said. "So. How's it going?"

The way he said it and the look he gave me—he knew something. We'd been friends too long for him to try to fool me.

158

"What do you know?"

"What do you mean?" he asked. "Hey, why are you here, anyway?"

"I need our house key. I'm locked out."

"Oh. I guess you left your bag at the salon, huh?" The pained look on his face was too much, like I was someone who'd just been diagnosed with terminal stupidity.

"Goldman, you better spill it. I'm not in the mood for these sad looks and questions that you're—"

"Okay, okay, fine. I just got off the phone with Eve."

Swallowing hard I asked, "Why'd she call you?"

Jonah shrugged, like they talked on the phone every day. Maybe they did. I guess they'd progressed from the texting stage. "She said she just needed someone to talk to and she couldn't talk to the one person she wanted to talk to—you. That's what she said. So she called to tell me—or just someone, I guess—what happened." I couldn't even look at him. I was so embarrassed and panicked over what I'd done—the stylists would think I was crazy for what I tried to do, and Mom and Eve would never forgive me for doing it. There was no getting out of trouble this time.

"She said you colored her hair, which I totally didn't believe at first, but when she said you colored it blue I realized that if anyone would do something as crazy as that, it'd be you. Dude, what were you thinking?"

I tried to swallow the lump in my throat. I'd seen the color washing down the sink but had clung to a tiny bubble of hope that it hadn't actually turned her hair *blue*. "I was just trying to give her some highlights. It's not like I set out to color it blue." I felt stinging behind my eyes, and my nose began to run as I tried my hardest not to cry.

"Oh, come on," he said, seeing what I was about to do. "I mean, it's not like you made her go bald or anything." He was still trying to tease me, but it sent me into overdrive. I sank down on his floor and let myself bawl. "Oh, great," he said, sitting down beside me. I don't know many guys who like to have a crying girl in their presence, but I couldn't help it. This was big.

"It's not funny," I stuttered through hiccuping tears. "Eve is supposed to do that commercial *tomorrow*. What if I ruined it for her?"

Jonah's voice softened when he said, "Yeah, she told me about that—about tomorrow."

"What else did she say?"

He didn't look at me as I wiped away the tears. "She was waiting to do her fitting and was worried about what Kitty would say."

"Bunny."

"Right. She also said your mom looked at her hair

160

but decided that she couldn't color it back to normal today because you jacked it up so bad. She said it's really fried. That's something to be proud of, isn't it?"

"Stop it, Jonah!" I said. "It's not funny."

He shrugged. "Maybe it is. Did you ever think of that?"

"No, I haven't. And I doubt Eve has, either." I knew he was just trying to calm me down and look on the bright side, but it wasn't going to work. "I have no idea how I'm going to fix this. What am I going to do? Hey," I said, swatting his knee with the back of my hand. "Think of something like you did for Be Gorgeous. That was practically your idea."

"Sorry, Mick," he said, and he seemed genuinely sorry—for me, maybe, or for Eve's situation. "I don't know anything about hair. All I know is that Eve is pretty upset and you should call her."

How could I even begin to apologize? Her hair was already ruined, and I was sure I wouldn't be allowed within a half-block of anyone's hair for the rest of my life.

I cried it out while Jonah sat awkwardly beside me, sort of ignoring me but at the same time letting me know he was there. Once I'd calmed down, he got me our house key and I went home. By the time I got to my room, I knew two things for sure: One, I had to make things right with Eve, and two, I had to accept the fact that I'd never be allowed to set foot in Hello, Gorgeous! again.

Upstairs in my room, I tried to come up with a solid plan of fixing some part of the disaster I'd created. I sat on my floor, trying to think, but all I could see was Eve's crying face and hear her voice asking Mom over and over, "What did she do?"

Things had been going so well with Eve and the other girls. I thought of my first sleepover and how much fun we'd all had doing makeovers. Now they were having sleepovers without me.

That reminded me of something. Something I'd seen the night of the sleepover in *Le Look*—that layout with the models I said looked like Eve. At the time I'd thought they looked like robots, but come to think of it, they actually looked more like aliens.

I grabbed the thick magazine off the bottom shelf of my bookshelf (*Le Look* wasn't something you threw away) and opened it to the alien spread. The crisp silver of the models' makeup had a cool, steely look and reminded me of the aliens in the game. That's when I knew I had an idea. It was farfetched, but I had to try something.

I threw open my closet door and starting digging like a dog at the beach. I had some old stuff from Halloween I hadn't used in a while that would be perfect. I threw the products I thought I could use on the floor behind me, not even paying attention to where they landed until I tossed back a glitter tube and it made a strange, dull thud. I turned to see that I'd nailed Mom in the leg. She stood behind me, glaring, the veins in her forehead pulsating.

"Never," she began, "in all my years! Have I ever! Seen something! So unbelievably! Irresponsible! And downright! Liable! In my entire! Life!"

Even though I was expecting to be seriously yelled at, it was still a jolt to be on the receiving end of all that. Mom raged on about what a mess I'd created and how there was no scenario in which she'd ever let me come back to the salon. I tried to tell myself that even though I didn't think I would ever work at the salon again, I could still fix things with Eve. I could try, at least. It might very well end up being the hardest thing I've ever done, but since when do I turn down a challenge?

CHAPTER 18

Even though I was still shaking from Mom's tirade, I tried calling Eve, knowing it was better to jump right in than to put it off and wait for my mind to come to its senses. Every time I dialed her number, though, it went straight to voicemail. She was screening my calls. I couldn't blame her, but I also wasn't going to give up that easily. Dad once said that a sign of maturity is figuring out how to solve your own problems, and that's exactly what I was going to do.

Sunday morning I went downstairs to Mom's office. I wanted to use the computer to find out where the commercial was shooting. Mom was just coming out. I froze when I saw her. Last night her face had been full of anger at me; this morning, it was something closer to regret. And mountains of disappointment.

"What is it, Mickey?" she asked as if I suddenly needed permission to go into her office.

"Is it okay if I check something on the computer for a minute?" I asked, my voice shaking.

For a moment she didn't say anything. "Make it quick," she finally said.

I watched her walk away down the hall, dressed for work, her heels clicking on the hardwood floors. She'd never been so icy to me before, hardly standing to look at or talk to me. It made me sick to my stomach. It made me start to reconsider my plan. I knew Mom wouldn't approve—today she wouldn't approve of me doing anything other than sitting quietly in my room and thinking about what I had done. But I really felt like I could not only fix things with Eve, but maybe help Mom understand why I'd done it in the first place. Maybe.

I went into the office and logged onto the computer. I was pretty sure Eve had mentioned that the commercial was being shot at a warehouse in town. I checked the local news sites, thinking maybe they had reported on it, then I Googled Bunny Jenkins. I found an interview she'd done for Warpath of Doom, and—*bam!*—she mentioned they'd be shooting at the warehouse at the end of Camden Way.

I gathered up all the makeup and supplies I'd found last night and put them in a plastic toolbox I never used because I never exactly had a reason to travel with a makeup kit . . . until now, anyway.

Mom hadn't actually told me I was grounded. I guess it was kind of understood, but she hadn't said the words. It was that tiny loophole that gave me a fraction of hope that I could leave home for just a little while and go for a stroll that just might take me to the warehouse. Once I heard Mom's car leave the driveway, I made a run for it.

"Bye, Dad! Going for a walk!" I yelled to him somewhere in the house. Then I quickly closed the front door behind me. I had just snuck out of the house for the first time in my life.

I didn't know what time the commercial would start shooting, but I hoped I'd get lucky—and I did. From two blocks away I could see white trailers lining the street and tons of people—some were standing around, some were carrying equipment into the old warehouse. People in all-white bodysuits with powdered-pale faces and white slicked-back hair walked around the set, and I assumed they were aliens. But then I spotted someone standing alone off to the side. This particular alien was dressed in the same white bodysuit but was wearing a Red Sox baseball hat, her hair tucked up inside. I recognized that hat. It was Jonah's. I felt a shock of anxiety, knowing that if she were wearing that ratty hat, her hair must be worse than I thought.

I started toward Eve and when she saw me, she

started shaking her head and backing away like I was coming after her with an ax—or a pair of scissors.

"Eve, come on. Wait," I called.

"I can't deal with you now, Mickey," she said, still slowly backing up. She looked over her shoulder as if checking her getaway strategy.

I picked up speed before she could run off. "Please! I just want to help." At first I thought she was going to spring off in the other direction, but she didn't. She suddenly came back at me with equal force, storming toward me. I stopped in my tracks, bracing myself.

"You ruined everything!" she said, a blue vein bulging in her forehead. "Everything was fine when I was being dressed in wardrobe—I actually thought I could get away with this." She pointed to her hat-covered head. "But then Bunny took one look at my hair and acted like I was some creature who had just crawled out of the sewer. It was like she couldn't even speak except to tell me to leave the hair and makeup trailer immediately."

"Oh my gosh, Eve . . ."

"She was all, 'Eve, why would you do that to yourself?' And what was I supposed to say? That I was stupid for letting you get anywhere near me? You streaked my hair *blue*."

As angry as she was, she also looked like she was on the verge of crying. "I have an idea!" I cried.

"Oh, that's super," she said. "Since your ideas always turn out so great."

It was like a good old-fashioned *pow!* Right in the kisser! That comment stung. I *did* have some good ideas. Hello—Be Gorgeous, anyone?!

Eve had every right to be mad at me. So I sucked up my own hurt feelings and said, "Eve, I'm so sorry about your hair. If I could take my own hair and put it on your head, I totally would."

She looked at me like she was actually considering something along those lines. "You're sorry?" she said. "Do you have any idea what's going on here? Yesterday when I finally made it to my fitting—which I was late for, by the way—I was able to keep my hat on and Bunny wasn't around. No one noticed a thing. But today—I can't believe I even bothered showing up. Complete disaster!"

"I know, Eve. But listen, I think I can help."

"My hair is *blue*," she said. "Even your mom couldn't fix it because she was afraid my hair would disintegrate or something if she tried."

"But maybe we can use that hair color to your advantage," I tried, opening my tool kit to show the magazine pictures I'd brought.

"Mickey, you're not getting it. They're not letting me be in the commercial anymore. They hired me partly because of my blond hair, and how white it was. *Was*," she stated, angrily brushing tears away. "I was really excited about being in this commercial. But now it's all a bust, so thanks a lot." She sniffled, wiped her nose, and looked longingly at the actors who were still part of the commercial. "Could you please just leave me alone, Mickey?"

Eve looked so sad and so defeated, like there was nothing left to do. "But I really think I can—"

"Mickey, seriously," she said. "I don't want you here. It's only making this worse. *Please go.*"

The toolbox in my arms felt as heavy as a box of new shampoos and conditioners. Tears welled up in my own eyes, and as I stood there looking at what I'd done to Eve—and I don't mean just her hair—I slowly realized that my plan was hopeless. What I'd done was too big, a true disaster. Maybe it was best if I just stayed away from everyone for the next five years or so.

"Okay," I said. "I just—I'm really sorry, Eve."

She didn't look at me as I turned and walked off.

As I left the set, I told myself that I had at least tried to make things right. I could feel good about that. Right?

Except I didn't. Walking away from the warehouse toward home, I felt like a huge failure—both as a wannabe stellar stylist and as a wannabe super friend.

CHAPTER 19

As I trudged toward home, I thought about how my chances of becoming a stellar stylist were long gone. But maybe, I thought, maybe there was still a way for me to be a super friend. Eve may have given up on me, but I hadn't given up on her—not yet, anyway.

I raced back to the warehouse. I found Eve right where I'd left her, except now she was sitting on the ground. Just sitting there in a patch of dirt. She looked so sad and alone. I felt awful times a thousand.

I thought she'd spring up and run away when she saw me, but she didn't. Maybe she didn't have the energy anymore.

"Eve, please listen," I said, my stomach a jumble of nerves. I sat down beside her. "If I promise I will not touch your hair, will you let me try my idea?" She looked at me through narrow eyes. "Can I at least show it to you?"

She considered me. "Fine. Show me. But that's all."

At least it was a start. I set down my tool kit and opened it up. "So listen. You're supposed to be an alien, right?"

"*Was* supposed to be," she said.

"Remember when I showed you this magazine when you all slept over?" I tried to ignore the pang of hurt caused by the hangout I wasn't invited to. Her eyes flickered to me, and she nodded. "Let's make you the best-looking alien here," I said. "Not some ghost alien like the rest of the actors, but something bigger than that, something more beautiful. See?" I handed her *Le Look*, the layout marked with yellow stickies. As she looked through the pages, I pulled all the shimmery, shiny, silver metallic makeup I had out of my toolbox—from eye shadows and blushes to lipstick and even this really cool silver mascara. "Okay, so your hair has some blue in it. But who said aliens can't be blue? Hello, what about *Avatar*? Um, can I see it?" Eve slowly reached up and pulled off the Sox hat.

Her hair wasn't as bad as I thought. I mean, okay, it was blue. But it was streaked blue and the shade was actually sort of pretty, like the fancy sparkling water bottles Mom keeps stocked. I could see how a person wouldn't want to wear this look every day, but on a special occasion—say, an alien commercial—it looked kind of cool.

I reached out to touch her hair, but Eve pulled back. "Don't touch. You promised!" She quickly pulled the Sox hat back on her head, and I couldn't resist asking.

"Can I—is that Jonah's?"

Her face softened the slightest, tiniest bit. "Yes. He let me borrow it the other day after school when my ponytail elastic broke. I forgot to give it back to him."

I smiled. "Forgot?" Because maybe she'd purposely forgotten, if you know what I mean. She didn't smile back. "Okay," I sighed. "How about if I just do your makeup? I can't permanently scar you with makeup . . . I don't think."

She looked at me carefully, then back at the magazine in her hand. "Okay. Fine. Makeup only."

I got to work applying a light-colored base that had only the smallest hint of shimmer, and then ramped up the look on her eyes. I wiped a straight swath of white eye shadow on her cheeks and topped it off with blue glitter. It was like pop-star overkill meets glam rock.

"Um, can I at least brush your hair out?" I asked.

"Give me the brush," she said, taking the hat off once again. "I'll do it."

Once her hair was brushed out and the makeup was done, I handed her a mirror so she could check out her new look.

"Wow. I didn't know glitter could look so spacey," she said.

"So," I said, "you like it?"

A smile washed over her pale, sparkly face. "Yes. I do. Mickey, this is actually really cool." I let out a deep breath. "What's that?" She pointed to the blue glitter hair spray on the ground that I'd wanted to use on her but couldn't bring myself to ask.

"I just thought a little blue glitter against your hair color would really pull the look together, but it's probably too much . . ."

"Hand it over," she said, putting the mirror down.

After she lightly sprayed her hair, she checked herself again in the mirror. "It's bizarre, but in a really amazing way." She looked past me to the crew closer to the warehouse. "I'm going to go find Bunny and show her. Who knows—maybe she'll like it. I mean, what do I have to lose at this point?"

"Do you want me to go with you?"

"That's okay," she said. "I don't know how she'll react if she sees non-commercial people on the set. Might be a rule or something."

"If you're sure. But I feel like I should go since, you know, this is all my fault. I could explain to her about what happened at the salon."

Eve smiled. "Listen, I'm not mad at you anymore, even though what you did to me was uncool, not to mention scary. I know you didn't mean to do it. I shouldn't have let you do it in the first place, but really you should never have suggested it."

"I know," I said. "I really am sorry."

"I know. We're okay now, right?" I nodded a grateful yes. Eve stood up. "I feel like I'm going in for my audition all over again. Except this time I really want it instead of just being curious."

"It'll be great," I said, standing up with her. "It has to be—you're the most ferosh alien I've ever seen, no matter what color your hair is."

Eve smiled. "Thanks, Mickey."

As I watched her walk off, determined to face Bunny, I took a deep breath and wondered what the odds were that I had helped her instead of making things even worse. I sat down on the curb to wait and find out.

CHAPTER 20

It felt like hours but was really only fifteen minutes later that Eve came out of the warehouse with her head down and a clipped pace to her step.

"Are you okay?" I asked, standing up to meet her. She couldn't even look at me. She couldn't even talk. "What'd she say? Eve, are you okay?"

She finally looked up at me as a huge smile spread across her face. "Bunny loved it! She took one look at me and said it was amazing. Just what she wanted, only she didn't know it until she saw it."

"Are you kidding?"

"She wants all the aliens to have this blue and silver look, even the boys—a variation of it, anyway. Mickey," she said, grabbing the sides of my arms. "You're a genius. You did it!"

Before I could start jumping up and down and celebrating, Eve said Bunny wanted everyone in

177

makeup stat so she had to go. "They're redoing mine a bit. I'm sure it's no offense or anything, but they're just going to touch it up some." Like I cared? No way! I hadn't ruined Eve's shot at commercial stardom! "A couple of assistants are being sent off to get silver and blue hair spray and some more shimmery makeup. Do you mind if they borrow yours to get started?"

Wait a minute. I'd realized something pretty awesome: They were going with my idea. *My* idea. *Whoa.*

"Take it," I said, handing my plastic toolbox over to her. "Use as much as you want!"

"Thanks, Mickey," Eve said, taking the case from me. "You saved the shoot."

I was absolutely positive I'd never met anyone nicer than Eve in my entire life.

I decided to hang around the set, since my only other option was to go home and have Dad put me to work doing some heinous chore like scrubbing mildew with a toothbrush. I did, however, think I'd better call Dad and let him know where I was. When I told him, instead of demanding I come home immediately, he calmly said, "I just got off the phone with your mother. She wants you at the salon. I think you'd better head over there."

Now that was something I didn't mind doing. After thinking Mom would never let me through those doors again, I practically ran the whole way there. Maybe somehow word had gotten to her about what I'd done on set and she wanted to thank me for my genius eye and tell me that all the top clients were now requesting *Mickey's* blue alien look.

Not exactly. The stern look on her face when I ran into her office definitely said her feelings toward me hadn't changed.

"Have a seat," she said. I sat in the chair opposite her, catching my breath. "I hear that you think the proper thing to do after the stunt you pulled yesterday is to go skipping around town without a care in the world."

I knew that leaving home had been a huge risk before I'd even stepped one foot out our front door. Part of me even knew I'd get busted for it. But it had to be done and the truth was I didn't regret it. How could I? Eve was back in the commercial. She had forgiven me. Of course, I didn't tell Mom this.

"Dad said you took off out of the house without permission, and since he's running around doing errands today, I thought you should stay here and work as well. That way I can keep an eye on you."

I almost leaped out of the chair and wrapped my arms around her. As long as Mom still allowed me to work in the salon, my chances of becoming a stellar stylist couldn't be too far gone. "You'll start in here," she said, "away from the clients. First you'll file these bills, according to date and company." She dropped a stack in front of me along with a box full of file folders. After that, she said I had to clean her office—sweep, mop, dust, straighten. "And when you're done with all this, I'll give you your next assignment."

Later as I was dusting the shelves, I heard a bit of a commotion up front. I peeked out the door and down the hallway to see what was going on. Eve was at the front with her mom and Megan was talking excitedly to Eve, touching her hair and looking her over with a big grin on her own face. Mom went up, and then Giancarlo and Devon, and soon half the salon was there, all fawning over her. It must have been because she was now an official star. I was so happy I hadn't ruined it for her. And maybe now Mom would see what I had done—the good stuff, the styling stuff. She'd finally understand why I'd done what I'd done to begin with, and maybe would even forgive me.

Eve spotted me lurking and waved me up. Mom hadn't said I couldn't show my face, so I headed up to say hi and see how the shoot went.

As everyone talked around us, she motioned me off to the side a bit.

"So," she asked, "are you in big trouble?"

I nodded. "Monster big. Mom hasn't given me the exact layout of my punishment yet, which means she's really thinking it over—it's going to be bad. Maybe by high school I can go out again."

"But you have to be un-grounded by this weekend," Eve said, her pale, sparkly alien face staring back at me. "The Warpath people are having a huge party on Friday where they're going to screen the commercial."

"Seriously?" I said. I may have fixed Eve's hair and makeup for the commercial, but I'd completely ruined things for myself. I'd never see daylight again. But I tried to be upbeat for Eve. "Sounds like a real Hollywood premiere."

"I know, that's what I was thinking," Eve said. "They gave me a bunch of passes, so I thought I'd invite everyone and we could all get dressed together. Think there's any chance you'll be off the hook by then?"

"Doubtful," I said, looking to my mom, who was still talking to Eve's mom.

Eve got this pouty little look on her face that made me feel even guiltier about not being able to be there for her. She looked at our moms, still talking. "Maybe my mom can talk to your mom and explain that there are no hard feelings?"

"I'm pretty sure there's no good explanation for me coloring your hair on my own."

"Yeah," she said. "I guess."

"Listen," I said. Now that this crisis had blown

over—and there were no burning hair dyes to distract Eve—I had to ask her about the other night. If Kristen was seriously still mad at me then I had a lot more to fix. "I wanted to tell you, I didn't have to have dinner with my parents. Kristen just didn't invite me to her house."

"You mentioned that when you were, you know, burning my head." I cringed, but she said, "Just teasing. But honestly, I can't believe Kristen would purposely not invite you."

"I'm pretty sure she did," I said. "I think she's still burned from how I handled our night at the mall."

"Yeah, but I was part of that, too," Eve said. "I was the one you went with."

"But you weren't the one who lied to her and Lizbeth about it," I said. "You didn't do anything wrong."

"I guess so, but still. I really thought she'd invited you, and you had plans. And honestly, I think Lizbeth thought that, too. I'm sorry, Mickey," Eve said. "Want me to help you talk to them about it?"

"That's okay," I said. "I messed everything up. I have to fix it."

"Just make sure you do it before my big premiere," Eve said. "Everyone has to be there. Including you."

"I'll work on making up with Kristen, but seriously—don't hold your breath. I have no idea if I'll be able to go."

With another apology in the works plus figuring out how to ace my oral report—not to mention suffering through all the punishment Mom was throwing my way—I was going to be pretty busy.

"Honey, you look outstanding," Giancarlo told Eve, stepping into our little conversation and twirling her around. "Simply stunning. Where was this commercial shot? Paris? You're out of this world!"

"That was the idea," Eve said, glancing my way with a grin.

Mom said, "You really do look incredible, Eve. They did a great job with your hair, and the makeup is flawless. Together, the whole look really works."

"Well, I'm glad you're impressed," Eve's mom said, "because your daughter did it."

I could feel myself blush at the compliment. "Did she?" Mom said, turning her eyes to me. I felt a flash of hope, but as Mom looked at me, she didn't look impressed. Not in the least. In fact, I wondered if she looked angry. The way her eyes cut through me, I couldn't be sure.

"Yes," Mrs. Benton said. "She came to the set and did this to Eve, and the casting director and director liked it so much, they did it to the other actors. Incredible, isn't it?"

Mom locked her eyes on me. She didn't agree with Mrs. Benton. She didn't even respond to her question.

She just gave her a tight smile and looked back at Eve. "Well," she said, "of course I'll personally fix your hair, honey. Get you back to your naturally gorgeous color." I felt the hope I'd been holding on to slink away. Mom wasn't impressed at all with what I'd done. In fact, I wondered if it made her even more upset with me. "How does your scalp feel?"

"Feels fine now," Eve said.

Mom inspected her head. "Looks like the irritation has gone away. If you're sure it feels okay, then come on back. We'll make this right. And Mickey?" she said, turning to me. "Have you finished the project you started in my office?"

"Not yet," I said. I headed back before she could punish me even more for getting involved in Eve's commercial—and going there in the first place. Eve gave me a sympathetic look as my mom led her to her station.

CHAPTER 21

An hour later I emerged from Mom's sparkling clean office, exhausted and dusty. I was about to head to the break room to get a drink and wash up when Mom came back. She'd just walked Eve out. I didn't even get to see how she looked.

"All finished?" Mom asked. I nodded yes. "Lizbeth has already started on the basement. It's sweet that she volunteered to clean it out, but I'm certainly not going to make her do it alone." Mom must have seen the confusion on my face because she said, "Go down and help her."

I dragged my tired legs down the metal staircase to the recent hair-horror scene. I spotted Lizbeth around the corner, dragging a box across the floor.

She stopped and looked over at me. "What are you doing here?" It almost sounded like an accusation.

"Punishment for Eve's hair," I said.

"So I guess your punishment is something I'm doing voluntarily." She turned her back on me and shoved the box across the floor with her foot.

Okay, so she clearly didn't want to talk to or even look at me. I wasn't sure that I wanted to talk to *her*, considering she may have told on me. Was she still so mad that she'd do something that low? And besides, how many ways could I say I was sorry about the mall? How much guiltier could I feel? I wanted to say, *Let's just get over this already,* but it seemed clear she didn't want to hear me say much of anything right then. Still, I knew I had to try because that's what friends do.

"I don't know how you're not freaked to be down here alone," I said. I figured acting casually, trying to be normal, would be a good start. "Try doing a dye job here. The whole scene was like something out of the *Saw* movies."

Lizbeth heaved the box she'd been shoving up onto a countertop and walked back to another one not far from me. She still didn't say anything, and I was pretty sure this was a classic silent treatment. I wasn't sure I deserved it, though. I mean, yeah, I had the mall thing against me, but if she was the one who got me busted, then that might trump things.

"So what's your system here?" I asked.

She looked in a box and pulled out an old round brush covered in hair. She dropped it back in, a disgusted look on her face. "It's worse down here than I thought." She looked around at the mess surrounding us in the dim light of the basement.

"I'm pretty sure there are various bugs and possibly mice living down here," I said.

"Probably."

The fact that she responded gave me a little relief.

I dragged the big trash can to the center, then went to one of the boxes that was already on the counter. "Are you just throwing away anything that's remotely sketchy?" She nodded. I lifted the box and dumped its contents in the trash.

Of course I wanted to make up with Lizbeth. She was my friend, after all. But I knew that before I even attempted to get there, I had to know why she'd told on me. Why would a friend do that to another friend?

"Why did—" I began. "Why did you want to clean this place out?" Argh, totally chickened out on asking the real question!

"I think it has potential and I thought your mom would appreciate the help," she said. She turned to look at me from across the basement. "What's wrong with that?"

"Nothing. It's really nice, I mean." Clearly I had to ask her, but I was afraid of what she might say.

"Look, did you . . . okay, did you tell on me yesterday?" It came out faster and harsher than I wanted, but I had to know.

"Excuse me?" She sounded defensive and she planted her hands on her hips.

"When Mom came down here when I was doing Eve's hair. I don't believe she just happened to come down here right at that moment. She hasn't been down here in months. And you were the only one who knew we were here."

"You think I would tell on you?" she snapped.

"I don't know," I said. "But you've been so mad at me about the mall trip—maybe you're getting back at me or something."

"Oh, please," she said, narrowing her eyes at me. "I don't care that much about you and Eve going to the stupid mall. And I didn't mean to tell on you, okay?"

"So you did tell?" I asked, stunned.

"Look, it was an accident." She bit her lower lip and finally looked up at me. "Your mom can be kind of scary sometimes, in case you didn't notice."

No argument here . . . I could tell she was upset, so I tried not to sound so angry when I said, "So what happened then?"

"It's not like I was tattling on you or trying to get back at you, okay? It wasn't like that."

"Okay," I said. "Then what was it like?"

"Well," she began, "yesterday your mom was at the front desk talking to some clients when Giancarlo came up, asking where Eve was. He was scheduled to give her that deep conditioning. I tried not to answer because I didn't want to lie—thanks a lot for putting me in that position, by the way. When your mom saw what time Eve's appointment was for and how long she'd been gone, she asked where you were. I tried to play it off and not answer her at all, but she could tell something was up. All I told her was that I thought I saw you guys go into the break room. I really thought she'd just leave it at that and wait for you to come back. I guess it was dumb to think she wouldn't go looking for you."

I felt sick to my stomach knowing I'd put Lizbeth in that situation. Being stared down by Chloe Wilson wasn't exactly something I'd like any of my friends to deal with. It's a pretty bleak experience.

"I get it," I said. "Totally and completely get it. I shouldn't have put you in that position in the first place. And I shouldn't have assumed you ratted me out. I'm sorry," I said.

"So," Lizbeth said. "Is that the only reason you were upset with me? Because you thought I told on you?"

"Truthfully?" She nodded, seeming to know there was more to it than what I'd said. "I was jealous at how easily you fit in here, not to mention that you did way better than me on the written report." She gave me a questioning look, so I said, "I heard you got an A on it. Did you hear what I got?" She shook her head no. "I got a C. I felt like I should have been the one doing great with the Career Ex thing, but you totally blew me away. You make, like, no mistakes. Ever."

Lizbeth crossed her arms as if I'd offended her. "I do so make mistakes. Once I brought a lady a regular soda instead of a diet. When she sipped it and realized it was regular, she snapped that I'd just ruined her seven-year streak of only drinking diet."

I couldn't help but laugh. "Do I have to remind you that I not only almost blinded a woman but I also almost made Eve go bald?" This made her smile. "I think that trumps a little aspartame. I don't want you to be mad at me, but I get why you are, okay?"

"I'm not mad, just hurt," Lizbeth said. "I was really excited about working at the salon. I thought we'd have so much fun together. At first I thought I was just being too sensitive about how you were acting. Then I felt like you ditched me to go out with Eve—not that I care if you guys do stuff without me and Kristen, but the fact that you lied about it made me feel like you were trying to avoid us."

"Kind of like how you guys ditched me Friday night at Kristen's?" I said. I hadn't planned on bringing that up—at least not that bluntly—but to be honest, it felt good. We had to talk about it.

Lizbeth, though, turned a little green. "Mickey, that was totally Kristen's idea. She said you had plans with your parents, but I got the feeling that wasn't true. I'm so sorry I didn't say anything to you about it."

"It's okay," I said, a lump forming in my throat. "Actually—it was really mean."

She nodded. "I know. It was. I guess I never believed that you had plans and just couldn't make it—I just chose to buy it to make myself feel better. But I should have stood up to Kristen, even though she was so angry. I'm really sorry. Can you forgive me?"

"Of course," I said. I meant it, even though I was still sad about everything that had gone down. I realized I still had very little idea how to be a good friend to girls. "Besides, I guess we don't always have to do everything together."

"But I like it when we all hang out," Lizbeth said. "Kristen does, too. That's why she was so upset about you and Eve not inviting us to the mall with you. You have to talk to her about it."

"I will," I said, feeling exhausted from all the stuff I still had to fix. "Are we okay, though? Or do I need to do something to make it up to you? I could color your hair?"

She laughed and grabbed the ends of her hair. "Not even! I'd rather clean this place up by myself than let you come near my hair with a bowl of hair dye."

"Why *did* you volunteer to clean this stuff out, anyway?" I asked.

"I guess I just like being here," she said. "I've had fun and I didn't want it to end."

"Hey, you never said—how'd the thing with the guys at the country club go last night?"

"It was kind of pretty much awesome." Lizbeth grinned. "I got there late but still in time for the barbeque. The four of us hung out a little bit, when the guys weren't getting yelled at for running onto the golf greens."

"So, does that mean you might be going out with Matthew?"

Lizbeth blushed. "Maybe."

"I'm really glad it worked out," I said. I looked around the basement—it didn't look like much progress had been made. But we had definitely made progress of our own. "Well, let's get down to it and show this mess who's boss! This place gives me the creeps."

"Agreed," Lizbeth said.

We decided to move all the boxes and junk from

the corners toward the center of the basement where the light was brighter and we could better see what was in them. After shuffling some smaller items away from the wall, we reached back together to drag a particularly big box out of the corner. When I saw the black mass behind the box, my voice caught in my throat. When my eyes focused and I saw the mass *moving*, I screamed.

Lizbeth jumped and said, "What?" with a horrified look on her face.

"Bugs! Bugs!" I yelled as I grabbed Lizbeth's arm and pulled her away with me. We both ran screaming up the basement stairs, vowing never to go back down until someone else guaranteed it was a bug-free zone.

CHAPTER 22

That night, I had just gotten out of the shower when Mom called for me to come downstairs.

"Well," she began once I sat down in her office. "I, for one, have finally calmed down enough to have a civil talk about what happened. Have you?"

"Yes," I said, hoping this meant she wasn't going to scream at me again.

"Then maybe we can start by having you tell me what exactly has been going through your mind lately because, honestly, I'm at a loss here."

"I don't know" was the in-depth response I came up with.

She sighed. "I want you to do well at the salon, honey. I really do. But I can't believe you'd try to color Eve's hair by yourself. That was the single most reckless thing that's ever happened in my salon. Do you realize we could have been sued?"

"I just wanted to help," I mumbled. "It was really busy and Eve was in a hurry and—I don't know. I guess I thought I could do it."

"Color her hair? With professional tools and products?"

I felt so ridiculous that I wanted to cry. "Some people say I'm really good at hair stuff. I thought I could show you that I'm not really a screwup at the salon."

"Mickey, is that true?" Mom asked, concern growing on her face. "Do you think that I think that about you?"

"It's just that I've made so many mistakes and Lizbeth never made a single one, and you acted so happy to have her there that I just felt like—I guess I felt like you liked her more than me. At the salon at least." I started crying, finally unable to help myself.

"Oh, Mickey," Mom said, resting her hands on my knees. She leaned forward and looked into my eyes. "That couldn't be further from the truth. I like Lizbeth, and she has been a big help at the salon. But nothing—no one—can compare to my own daughter."

I wiped my runny nose, keeping my eyes on the floor.

"Sweetie," she said, her voice softening even more, "maybe it's because you're my daughter that I hold you to higher standards than anyone else. I know how much you love the beauty business and that it's something you want to do, maybe even as a career. You'll never know how happy that makes me."

"Really?" I said.

"Really. That's why I'm harder on you than I am on Lizbeth. Because I *know* you can be great at styling hair. And makeup, as it turns out . . . but you have to be patient and learn first—just like all the other professionals. And you've been doing great—well, until Eve."

"She's okay now, though. Right?"

"Her hair won't be falling out any time soon," Mom said, and she even cracked a little smile.

I wiped my nose and said, "I can't believe I did that. I don't know what I was thinking. Coloring is a lot harder than it looks."

"You may find this hard to believe," Mom said, "but we're actually trained professionals."

"I know," I said. "I promise I won't do anything that stupid ever again, Mom."

"I know, honey," she said, patting my leg. "Now, you have that oral report coming up for your Career Exploration class, correct?"

"Yes."

"Considering how you did on the written report and all that's happened since then, I expect great things on the oral section. How about we make a deal? If you get an A- or better, you can come back to work."

"You mean you're not firing me?"

"Not yet, anyway," she said, and actually cracked a grin. Mom reached over and hugged me. I hugged her back tight, taking in the fresh scent of her vanilla spice shampoo—our newest product.

"So—are you going to make me go back to that basement?"

"After you girls left I realized that the job is much bigger than I thought. And the exterminators will be called first thing tomorrow! I'll need to find someone else to either help with it or just hire a crew. Lizbeth had a great idea, but I don't think it's an appropriate job for you kids."

I nodded. I was relieved that things were finally settling back into place. Lizbeth had totally rocked it at Hello, Gorgeous!, and my mom thought I was doing well at the salon, too. I had no idea that she was proud of me and that she actually thought I had a future in the styling biz. Eve and Lizbeth weren't mad at me, and even though my job at the salon was still on the line, at least I knew what I had to do to get it back. The only thing left was Kristen. I'd saved the hardest part for last.

"Guess what?" Eve said as soon as I answered the phone later that night. "My commercial is done!"

"Really? I didn't know they could do it that fast."

"I know. And the filming went by fast, too. Mickey, it was *amazing*."

"I want to hear every detail. Spill!" I said, my stomach fluttering with excitement for her.

"This is going to sound dumb," she said, "but I felt like a movie star. There were, like, a hundred people running around on this crazy set inside the warehouse with dry ice and weird mountains, and even though I didn't have any lines to say, it was really hard to act like an alien. But Bunny called me a natural and said they loved working with me!"

"I'm so excited for you," I told her. "Do you think you'll do more acting stuff?"

"I don't know. Like Bunny said—and Kristen, who's apparently an expert on all things Hollywood—they hardly ever shoot anything around here. I'd have to go to Boston if I wanted to try to do more. It was fun, but I'm not sure I'm that into it. Mom would have to take time off work to drive me and everything. But it was still amazing, and the other kids who were in it with me were really cool, too."

"I'm so glad it all worked out," I said.

"Yeah," she said. "Me too. So what've you been up to?"

"Actually, I have good news. Lizbeth and I made up."

"Really?" she said. "That's awesome! What happened?"

"For some insane reason she decided to volunteer to help clean out that scary basement at the salon. We were basically trapped down there, so we had to talk it out."

"And what about Kristen? Everything okay with you two now?"

I groaned. "Not yet. But I'm working on it." I wasn't sure how yet, but I knew it was coming. "Oh! And I have *more* good news. Mom said if I get an A- or better on my oral, I can come back to the salon and I won't be grounded—which means there's still a glimmer of hope that I can go to your premiere."

"Oh my gosh, you *have* to ace that report," Eve said.

"I know," I said. "I have an idea that I think might work, but I'll need a little help." When I told her my idea she laughed, but in a good way.

"I think it's brilliant," she said. "Everyone is going to love it!"

I was relieved that a plan was in action. Now I could start working out the details. One by one, I'd set everything right again. I just had to.

CHAPTER 23

That week at school I pretty much chickened out on the whole Kristen thing. I don't know what it was about her, but I was more nervous than I was when I made up with Eve or Lizbeth. In one way I just wanted to get it over with, but then every time I saw her my stomach cramped up and I went mute. Plus, she and Lizbeth had started sitting at a different table at lunch. Lizbeth later told me she was sorry, that she didn't mean anything by it, but I understood, and I knew it was up to me to fix things. I had to concentrate on my oral report, but I swore I'd get to Kristen once it was over with. In the meantime, she stayed just icy enough to let me know she was still angry.

Ms. Carter had given the okay for Eve to help me perform my presentation. Eve had even come over on Wednesday night—when I would normally have been at the salon—to go over the final details.

On Thursday we all crowded into the Little Theater for our presentations. Kristen's radio station presentation was laced with sarcasm, and Eve, Lizbeth, and I sat in our chairs stifling laughs the whole time.

Eve's presentation was filled with pictures of the cute kids she looked after in the day care. It totally softened the teachers up—I mean, they were all *aaahhing* in unison. Totally benefited all of us who came after her. Such a pioneer.

Jonah seemed to have gotten more out of his job than he thought he would. He had even brought in some old toys, saying how they were made out of metal and not plastic so they were sturdier and lasted longer. Matthew talked about working in the pro shop and being a part of the country club team. And Tobias basically gloated about his job as bat boy with the Red Sox. Every guy in the theater was drooling over his presentation. Us girls rolled our eyes.

Kyle talked about life around the firehouse and said firefighters are the best cooks in the world. I could tell he was nervous speaking in front of the crowd because he kept pushing his hair off his forehead. He told us that there were no actual fires in Rockford while he was working there. "Well," he said, "except for the fire I started when the guys had me help grill steaks for dinner one night."

As for Lizbeth, she gave a very good, no-nonsense presentation. She talked about the business side of running a salon, how the stylists earn tips and keep their chairs at the salon as well as the complicated task of booking clients and how an otherwise regular basement could turn into a disaster zone.

Finally, it was my turn to present. Eve and I went up the side stairs and into the wings of the stage like we'd been told.

I got a chair from the side and dragged it to center stage with Eve beside me. I took the microphone from the stand, thinking of what Giancarlo had said to Piper about performing in front of a crowd—*picture yourself being fabulous, and fabulosity will follow.*

"Hello, gorgeous!" I yelled into the microphone.

Silence rang back at me. I tapped the top of the mic to make sure it was on. Sadly, it was.

"Um, well. Hi!" I said. "I got to work at my mom's salon which is called . . ." I leaned into Eve as planned and we both said, "Hello, Gorgeous!" This time we got a couple of pity chuckles. "Okay, so um, Eve is going to help me show what it's like to work at a salon and what I learned from the experience. Lizbeth already did a great job in her presentation of showing us the business side of things, didn't she? Way to go, Lizbeth!"

I visualized the crowd applauding Lizbeth and her

shyly waving from her seat. Instead no one applauded. I looked over at Ms. Carter and caught her checking her watch. Had I made a huge career-ending mistake by trying to be clever in my presentation?

"The first thing I learned when I started my job," I said, trying to get back on track, "is that being gorgeous takes a lot of work." Eve sat in the chair and I took out a plastic cape and wrapped it around her. Even though we'd never use plastic in the salon, it made for a better prop. "And you should never try to do beautiful things to other people unless you're, you know, qualified."

"Um, excuse me, miss," Eve said in her best *la-di-da* voice. "I'd actually like to *keep* my hair, thanks very much."

There were some laughs in the audience—word had spread about what I'd done to Eve's hair. It was all tied up in her being-in-a-commercial story.

"When you work at a salon, you should always be courteous to your clients," I said. "Offer them a beverage while they're waiting."

I offered her a bottle of water, then accidentally-on-purpose spilled it all over her legs as an ode to what I'd once done to Ms. Carter. "But don't spill it all over them!" Eve said, jumping up.

I glanced over at Ms. Carter and said, "Sorry!" I ran to the side to get my next prop. "You should be prompt with great customer service. But don't race through the salon because you could trip, fall, and possibly blind someone."

I pretended to trip and then tossed Eve a phony bottle labeled HAIR DYE with a skull and crossbones on it. She pretended it had spilled on her. She yelled and clutched her hands over her eyes. "I'm blind! I'm blind!" Eve was really working it. By now, people were getting more into it. I even saw Ms. Carter smiling.

"Pay attention to what your job is, not what other people are doing," I said.

"Um, Mickey?" Eve said, standing up and pointing to the floor. "Please put down the scissors and sweep up this mess."

We went on like this, mostly going over all the mistakes I'd made but turning them into jokes—I mean, *lessons*. Everyone seemed to enjoy it.

"And never," I said at the end, "no matter how *few* mistakes your friend—I mean, *co-worker*—makes, never resent her for that. Remember, you're a team, you're not in competition, and we all have room for improvement." I looked at Lizbeth. "And you should never punish anyone for doing what's right. And if you do, well—you should say you're sorry."

Lizbeth flicked her eyes back down. I couldn't tell if she was emotional or embarrassed or what. Trying to end on a light note I said, "Now! If anyone would like me to color their hair for free, step right up and . . ."

"Mickey!" Eve said, all exaggerated and right on script. "Have you not learned anything from this experience?"

"I'm only kidding." I looked back out at the audience and said, "Of course I'd charge for hair coloring!"

We ended our presentation with everyone laughing right along with us, including Ms. Carter. We took a bow. As I looked out at the audience, I locked eyes with Kristen.

Five million messes corrected, one more to go.

CHAPTER 24

After the presentations, Eve and I invited Kristen and Lizbeth to sit with us at lunch. Kristen shrugged as if she didn't care if she ever sat with—or talked to—us ever again, but Lizbeth said *of course* they'd sit with us.

"Mickey, that was awesome!" Lizbeth said as we sat down at our table. Jonah and Kyle were on the end. They were deep in their own conversation and not paying attention to us. "Yours was the best one, for sure."

"I think everyone did a great job," I said, looking at Kristen, who looked bored. "Kristen, your job didn't turn out to be so bad after all, huh?"

She looked off across the cafeteria and said, "I guess."

"Kristen," I said. I knew I had to fix everything, now. There was no more oral presentation prep to hide behind. Maybe being surrounded by my friends—the ones who weren't mad at me—would give me some strength. "Look, I know you're still mad about the whole mall-lying thing."

Kristen rolled her eyes. "I'm, like, so over that."

"Oh, puh-leaze!" Lizbeth said, practically laughing at her friend.

"I am!" Kristen said.

"And I know you invited everyone over last Friday night except for me," I said.

She looked right at me and said, "I thought you already had plans."

"Lies," Lizbeth said, shaking her head. "K, that is so not true and you know it."

Kristen looked embarrassed, but I knew she would stand her ground, at least for a little bit longer.

"Look, I'd be mad, too, if you had ditched me and lied like I did. And I was sort of mad about you leaving me out of things the other night," I said. "But I shouldn't have lied to either of you. And I'm really sorry."

"I told you," Kristen said, "I don't care about that stupid mall thing. *It's no big deal.*"

"Then what are you mad about?" Lizbeth asked her.

"It's just," Kristen began, then stopped and turned to Lizbeth. "Okay, fine. It's just that you and Mickey got to work together and Eve got this amazing commercial and, like . . ."

"Oh my gosh," Lizbeth said, and for a moment I thought she was going to start laughing. "You're jealous!"

"I am not!"

"You practically just said so," Lizbeth said.

"Whatever," Kristen said, but she sounded more hurt than angry. "I just felt a little left out, that's all."

"Well, we're all here now," Eve said. "Together!"

"I guess," Kristen said.

"Come on," I said. "I forgive you for not inviting me last Friday if you forgive me for lying about the mall. We can call it even. What do you say?"

Kristen sat quietly for a moment, until Lizbeth nudged her. Finally she looked at me and said, "Okay. That seems fair. So, look, I'm sorry about not inviting you on Friday and you're forgiven for lying. Just don't do it again."

"Really?" I said. "I'm forgiven?"

She smiled. "Totally and completely."

I felt relieved. Everything was finally getting back into place. "Now we can celebrate Career Ex ending *and* . . ." I looked at Eve pointedly. She blushed instantly. "Eve? Anything you'd like to share with the table?"

"Oh, I don't know," Eve said. She pretended to be

annoyed, but I could tell she was excited. "It's just that my commercial is done and I thought maybe it'd be fun for us all to see it together. If you guys care, I mean."

"Of course we care," I said. "We're your friends!"

"Well," she said, leaning in toward us with her back to Jonah and Kyle, who were still totally ignoring us, all into their own conversation. To me she said, "Remember how I told you I got free passes? Well, I thought we could *all* invite someone." She nodded behind her, indicating the boys.

"Like ask them to come with us?" I asked quietly so the boys wouldn't overhear. Even Kristen looked mortified at the idea—and she was the brave one.

"It doesn't have to be a date," Eve said. "I just think—hang on." She turned around to Jonah and said, "Hey, could you do me a favor? I'm totally craving some, uh, milk. Could you go get me a carton?" She got some money out of her bag and handed it to Jonah, who looked a little thrown off.

"Uh, yeah," he said. "Sure."

Jonah got up to leave and Kyle sat staring at us— like either we were crazy for not being able to get our own milk or because he was going to try to join in our convo while Jonah was on his mission. Eve nudged me.

"Oh, um, Kyle?" I said, digging in my bag for cash.

210

"Will you get one for me, too?"

"Sure," he said, looking at all of us like we'd gone insane. He took the money and headed off.

Once he'd gone, Eve leaned in to us again and, speaking quickly, said, "I just think it'd be fun if we all went together. Don't you guys think so?"

"You seriously want us to ask them out?" Lizbeth asked.

"Why not?" Eve said. "People do it all the time. Come on, don't be chicken." She turned to see the boys walking back to the table, each carrying a carton of milk. Was she really going to do it? I looked at Kyle, carrying my drink for me. I wasn't sure I could do it, even though I liked him and thought he was cute. As they sat back down at the table, I was attacked by a major case of the butterflies.

"Here goes," Eve whispered to us, and we all watched anxiously.

"Your majesty," Jonah said, bowing slightly as he handed her the carton of milk.

"Thanks," Eve said. "Hey, listen. I have this commercial premiere thing tomorrow night. And they'll be opening up the live-action game so you'd get to play after the screening. We're all going and it's free."

Jonah looked stunned for a moment and turned to Kyle for help. Kyle looked down at me, but I darted my eyes away. Finally Jonah said, "Yeah. Sure." Like it was no big deal. But I could tell it was.

"Cool," Eve said, then turned back to us, blushing but looking very pleased with herself. She nudged me under the table with her leg. "Go," she mouthed.

I glanced at Kyle. It would just be all of us hanging out. It wasn't that big of a deal. I took a deep breath and said, "Hey, Kyle. Want to go, too?"

A grin flickered across his face. "Sure," he said.

I leaned back toward the girls, feeling pretty fearless.

"You make it look so easy," Lizbeth said in a lowered voice, glancing two tables over to where Matthew and Tobias sat. Jonah and Kyle had already gone back to their own conversation, but I knew that this time they were just pretending to ignore us. I knew because Kyle's cheeks were still pink and Jonah kept glancing at Eve.

"It is easy," Eve said, matching Lizbeth's lowered tone. "You just *ask*."

"Maybe," Lizbeth said. "But no way are we doing it here."

"Okay," Eve said. "But you have to do it soon. The party is *tomorrow*."

"We will," Lizbeth said. "I promise."

※ ※ ※

After school I waited out front with Eve for her mom to come pick her up.

"Are you sure you don't want a ride home?" she asked. "We can drop you off on the way to my grandmother's."

"No, I'm good," I said. "Thanks, though."

The truth was, I hoped I could "run into" Ms. Carter on her way out so I could find out about my grade. She might not have made up her mind yet, but it couldn't hurt to ask.

A few minutes later when Eve's mom pulled up, Eve asked, "Want me to wait with you?"

"No, go ahead," I said.

"Okay," she said, walking backward toward the curb, "but I want every detail!"

I smiled and waved good-bye, then leaned against the building to wait.

It wasn't long before I spotted Ms. Carter walking out the school door and heading toward the teachers' parking lot.

"Ms. Carter," I called, running to catch up with her. "I was wondering about the grades for our oral reports."

"Hello, Mickey," she said, looking at me curiously. "I plan on handing those out on Monday."

"Okay. But, well, do you think you could maybe please let me know about my grade now? I know it's a lot to ask. And I wouldn't ask if it wasn't really *really* important."

She looked at me like she was thinking about it. "I heard through the grapevine what happened at the salon." That was the thing about hair salons and small towns—word always traveled fast. "I've given you an A on it. I hope that comes as good news to you."

I thought I would jump up and hug Ms. Carter right there in front of the entire school. Instead I acted all mature and said, "Thank you so much!"

She smiled. "It was well deserved. Have a good evening, Mickey."

I couldn't believe it. Everything was working out, right when I thought it couldn't. Somehow I'd scraped by, and now all I had to concentrate on was creating the perfect look for the premiere!

CHAPTER 25

We all met at Eve's to get dressed before the big opening on Friday. Eve, Lizbeth, and Kristen all cheered when I showed up, knowing that it meant I'd gotten a good grade on my oral report.

"Hey, you made it!" Kristen said. She smiled wide.

"Back to the salon, too, right?" Lizbeth asked.

"Yep!" I said. "Back to Hello, Gorgeous!"

"I knew everything would work out," Eve said.

I got busy fixing her hair. I did it in a half updo with piecey angles framing her face that made her look glam, but maybe like she was too cool to get *too* dressed up. She wore a white sleeveless blouse with silver sequins going down the front and white satin cargo pants. She looked like she was ready for the red carpet of a big-budget action movie.

I kept things simple by styling my hair in loose, natural curls and wearing a short dress with wedge sandals. I styled Kristen's hair in a messy low bun that still looked perfect, and once Lizbeth was dressed in a one-shoulder top with shredded jeans, we were ready to work the red carpet at Eve's big premiere.

"Are you nervous?" I asked Eve as I swiped on some lip gloss.

"Not really," she said. "Well, maybe a little. Hey, can I ask you guys something?"

"Shoot," Lizbeth said, finger-combing her hair in the mirror.

"Are you nervous? I mean about hanging out with guys?"

My stomach tightened thinking about it—but in a good way. "I'm nervous. But it's like you said—we're all just friends, hanging out."

"Yeah, but with guys. That's different," Eve said.

"I'm friends with Jonah. That's not different."

"You know what I mean," she said, and I did know. I also didn't want the pressure of being on an actual date, so I still wanted to just call them friends.

"I'm kind of glad I don't have to deal with that," Lizbeth said, "since we chickened out and never asked the guys."

"Lame," Eve said. Lizbeth had told us after school that they couldn't get the courage to do it. "You should be suffering right along with us."

Eve's mom called us, and it was time to go.

The event was a much bigger deal than Eve had let on. There were a ton of people and cars lined up, and the outside of the old warehouse had roaming spotlights swinging across the sky plus a real red carpet leading to the front. There were even some local photographers snapping pictures as people went inside.

When we pulled up to the curb we saw all four boys were waiting for us—or for Eve, who had their tickets—just outside the doors.

Lizbeth practically choked when she said, "Matthew is here? And Tobias?"

Kristen tried to act like it was no big deal when she said, "I slipped a note in Tobias's locker this afternoon and asked them both to come. Not as brave as Mickey and Eve, but it looks like my note got the job done."

"Wow," Lizbeth said. "Nice job."

The guys wore jeans but seemed a little more put-together than usual. Even Jonah's cowlick seemed to be behaving, and Kyle's curls looked a little crunchy, but one still fell over his eye so it was okay. And, okay, fine, he looked kind of cute.

Everyone said hey and then we went inside, where the scene was otherworldly. The two-story warehouse had been transformed into an alien planet with lots of white and silver and blue streaks. Dry ice floated across the floors and blue lights shone down from the two-story ceiling. I guess I'd been on the cutting edge when I accidentally colored Eve's hair. But Eve was right—it'd turned out perfect in the end.

Snacks were served by waiters in white jackets and we all loaded up as if we hadn't eaten since Monday. When they showed Eve's commercial, all seven of us cheered for her. She looked killer as a wide-eyed alien walking stealthily through a washed-out landscape while enemy spacecraft exploded around her.

"That was amazing!" I said once it had ended.

"Great job, Eve," Lizbeth said.

"Pretty cool," Jonah said. "But I bet I can beat you at this live-action thing." He jerked his thumb toward the game entrance. Eve said, "You're on," and took off without him.

"Hey!" he said, then followed after her. "Illegal start!"

We all laughed, then Kyle, Tobias, and Matthew looked at the rest of us.

Kyle stood near me with his hands shoved in his pockets.

"How about it, Lancaster?" I said to him. "Wanna go play?"

He grinned a dimpled smile. "You're on."

We took off running toward the entrance.

"Hey!" I heard Kristen's voice behind me. "Wait for us!"

We raced to the starting line, and I could hear everyone else running behind us—all my friends, together.

DON'T MISS THE FIRST BOOK IN THE SERIES!

Hello, Gorgeous!

Blowout

BY TAYLOR MORRIS

BOOK YOUR NEXT
APPOINTMENT WITH

Tangled

COMING SOON . . .

ABOUT THE AUTHOR

Taylor Morris is the author of several books including *Class Favorite* and *Total Knockout,* and her short stories and articles have appeared in *Girls' Life* magazine. She graduated from Emerson College in Boston, MA, and currently lives in New York City with her orchestra conductor husband. She does not get her hair cut in a fancy salon like Hello, Gorgeous!, but she loves hearing from her readers about their latest hairstyles and favorite names for both real and imaginary nail polish colors. Visit her at www.taylormorris.com and tell her your favorites!

Photo by Silas Huff